SUMMONING, SKATING, AND SKULLS

BEWITCHER'S BEACH PARANORMAL COZY
MYSTERIES
BOOK 2

EMILY FLUKE

ALSO BY EMILY FLUKE

Be sure to snag the prequels to both the Mari Fable Mysteries, and the Bewitcher's Beach Paranormal Cozy Mysteries FREE from my newsletter: The Glass Coffin and Be Careful What You Witch For.

https://landing.mailerlite.com/webforms/landing/y4h6c8

To everyone who wanted to grow up and become a member of the Charmed family, had a crush on Goliath from Gargoyles, Spike from Buffy the Vampire Slayer, or Casper from Casper.

CAST OF CHARACTERS

Noema Wolf (temporary last name. Once werewolves are turned they have no memory of their previous life):

As a werewolf who can smell emotions and a lover of mystery movies, Noema finds herself sniffing out suspects whenever a troublesome visitor upsets her cozy, seaside town. But another case is not what this single mother of four, manager of Mockbuster Video Rental, and playwright needs thrown into her busy schedule.

Halen, Dio, Jovi, and Stevie Wolf:

These four mischievous 'pups' each help their mom solve mysteries or run the video rental shop in their own unique ways. As born werewolves, they don't experience memory loss —but as eight-year-olds, they suffer selective hearing when it comes to following the rules.

Sheriff Sett Lawrence:

This overprotective gargoyle takes life too seriously. His six foot, six inch stony, body with muscular wings and horns, does nothing to match his introverted, patient, and studious personality. But it certainly frightens visitors.

Crow:

A mysterious man with a handsome smirk. Crow took advantage of the low housing market in Bewitcher's Beach after a newcomer was recently murdered. This "tall dark" has plenty of secrets but isn't afraid to tease, flirt, and joke in the face of danger. And as hidden as he may seem—as the new owner of Roller Shakes—Crow socializes with the whole town on a regular basis.

Mae Wildefyre:

Like her husband, Wallace, and other half-dragons, Mae resembles a human but has shiny, scaly skin. Before, when human hunters came after supernatural people, Mae hid with the other half-dragons, shifting herself to appear fully human. Now, she's the center of attention, and she loves it...until her secrets spread like wildfire.

Fate Kalabar:

A wild college kid visiting his family's vacation home during a break from Shadowvale University. His natural ease with magic allows him to pass classes with little study and a lot of partying. Often drunk and disorganized, Fate's fate is doomed before he can say "graduate."

Gemma Stone:

Serious, like her partner against crime. Gemma is Bewitcher's Beach's newest hire at the local police station. But she isn't new to Sett. Having once dated the sheriff, Gemma has a welcome invitation into town, though she doesn't exactly want to fit in.

Hattie Sharpe:

This harsh, flapper-girl starlet became a ghost in the height of the Roaring Twenties when her bold attitude landed her the target of a deadly Hollywood stunt. Now, she directs Everland Theater's plays and tells it like it is, no matter how many enemies it creates.

Bette Sharpe:

Hattie's teenage daughter. This ghost babysits the wolf kids for money to develop the film on her Kodak camera. What crime will her photograph's capture?

Senna James:

This young witch is about as stylish as she is skilled with magic. A current student at an out-of-town college, Shadowvale University, Senna is busy studying spells, dealing with class-mates, and flying away on her broom before her bad choices catch up with her...

Dr. Pitt:

While this werebulldog takes care of everyone else in town, who will help him overcome his nerves? What might make this gentle doctor so anxious anyway?

Mayor Fitz Feet:

As if summoned by his name, this short, shiny-headed mayor and volunteer police officer always appears with a cheerful countenance and a glass-half-full attitude. A leader of a town full of rumors, superstitions, and supernatural creatures must stay positive—even when a murder threatens to ruin Bewitcher's Beach's reputation. And his.

CAST OF CHARACTERS

Squeaks:

A mouse. Arrogant, intelligent, and adorable, but still just a mouse.

Ancestors of chosen witches will be marked, revealing the descendant.

Each chosen one offers protection with magic of intent.

One pirate, Annette, with skills of swords against every threat.

One mother, Midnight, with the protection of foresight.

One who weaves as a crafter, defenses for all that come after.

One who commands both winter and summer to split enemies asunder.

One with the power of scent to smell a threat's intent.

One with the language of fauna and flora to lead defenses against malevolent aura.

Each chosen for her skill, to shield innocents from those who kill.

Pirate.

Psychic.

Crafter.

Weathercaster.

Canine.

Communicator.

Each in a family with gifts to protect from every witch hater.

This is the prophecy of the Titan family.

CHAPTER 1
MADAM ROWENA'S DAY OFF

1997 COASTAL CALIFORNIA

A HEAVY WIND almost toppled the leaning tower of VHS tapes that precariously balanced on my forearms. Distant thunder threatened Bewitcher's Beach with a storm. The chill bit through my oversized argyle sweater and had me wishing to turn into my wolf form.

"Do you need help, Noema?" a deep voice asked.

I peered over the top of the video stack just in time to dodge a light pole and smile at an enormous gargoyle in my path. He flattened his leathery wings against the wall of the hair salon, clearing space on the sidewalk. The ornate black iron that curved beneath the frosty bulb almost snagged the curls on the top of my head. I ducked around the lamp post and carefully avoided the bumps in the cobblestone, a pathway I knew well. "Hi, Sett. I think I've got it thanks to my crew of helpers." I nodded at my children. Two trailed behind me, one followed at my side, and the last one bounded up front.

Sett greeted the kids with a high five, a fist bump, a quick hug, and a handshake. Each hello was unique to their personality. Since he took the time to get to know their preferences, the sheriff was one of my childrens' favorite people. I tempered my ridiculous grin when he looked at me. Though we never officially dated and we certainly wouldn't after he'd arrested me last month, I couldn't quell the butterflies his smile sparked.

"You should hurry and get those tapes inside before the rain gets here. Are you sure you don't want a hand?" He reached out in an offer to take the tapes. The sleeves of his police jacket were shoved to the elbows, exposing the corded muscles of his thick, stony forearms. I had to draw my eyes away before heat burned my cheeks.

The blustery day tossed dark curls into my face, and I had to blow the hair away before it got caught in my mouth. "I'm okay, but I'm worried about the roads. Will flooding postpone the witch?" After a murder only a few weeks earlier, the people of Bewitcher's Beach had learned that the town's legendary protection spell was not only real but had kept our supernatural community safe. Nobody knew exactly how the spell worked, but we knew it stopped danger in its tracks. When the magic had mysteriously unraveled, our only hope to restore the protection was a witch professor at Shadowvale University. Thankfully, my wolf's nose helped me sniff out a grimoire with the protection spell, and now all we had to do was wait for the talented witch to come cast it.

"Yes." Sett pinched his brow, and a crease formed between the horns on his forehead. "Madam Rowena was supposed to come as soon as the storm moved on. Now that it's headed straight for Bewitcher's Beach, the professor will have to wait. The roads into town are already flooded. According to the weather records, we haven't seen a storm this bad in decades. It'll definitely put a damper on the holidays," he said, referring to The Ghost Pirate Moon. Once every ten years, a ship came ashore and the spirits that haunted it visited their ancestors in town. I'd heard it was a huge reunion full of family, friends, and food.

2

I frowned as my eyes trailed past him to the dark windows of my shop. The red sign that hung in the window read "Mockbuster Video Rental." "I'd better get these to the roller rink," I said. Sett's eyes sparkled with questions as his gaze dipped to the tower of VHS tapes. "I struck a deal. The roller rink will play some of these older movies on their TVs, and hopefully, the viewers will come to Mockbuster to rent the sequels. Anyway, I've got to run."

"Me too." His voice was low, and his eyes shifted away as he hurried past me. Odd. Since Sett never walked quickly, anywhere. I tore my gaze from the wings at his back, knowing I didn't have time to dwell on it.

The walk from Mockbuster to Roller Shakes skating rink was one I could normally do with my eyes closed. But this time of year, holiday decorations added obstacles in my path. On the cusp of the Ghost Pirate Moon, locals went overboard with marine decorations. Anchors lined the sidewalk, blue lights strung from overhangs to lamp posts, and the tattered black fabric of faux pirate flags were strewn across windows. If I didn't trip over a plastic pirate skull, my curls tangled in the low-hanging string of lights. I opted to walk on the sidewalk's edge and employed my children to warn me of the next obstacle.

"Pirate flag!" Jovi shouted.

I froze and craned my neck to see around the tower and side-stepped a flag pole. My son shot me two thumbs up and then used one finger to shove the thick glasses higher on his nose. Other than the paws that replaced his human feet, Jovi looked more and more like his late father every day.

Stevie skipped along beside me, pigtails bouncing, while Halen and Dio dragged behind, too fixated on their handheld Game Boys to keep pace with us. Each pup carried a pair of skates strung over their shoulders, except for my daughter.

Stevie tucked the roller skates into her armpits and housed a pet in each one. Under her left arm, our pet mouse's tan whiskers poked out of the top of the skate's cushioned interior, and on the other side, the pinchers of a Dungeness crab clung to the laces. Squeaks glared at the crab.

"Mom!" Jovi shrieked, cutting through my thoughts.

Adrenaline swelled with the desperate pitch of my son's voice. Before I could think, my body reacted, dropping to all fours and shifting into my fastest and most threatening form. Now that I was a wolf, my clothes fell to the ground, and the VHS tapes clattered across the cobblestone. As soon as my brain caught up with the situation—Jovi was merely warning me of a sign in my path—I released a quick howl, and the smoky scent of frustration poured out of me. As always, my sharp nose couldn't help but catch the smell of emotions, my own or otherwise.

Jovi palmed his face at my dramatic reaction.

Since the murder, I'd become overprotective, and the transformation happened faster than a flick of my tail. When I heard my child in distress, I shifted, ready to battle the threat with my claws and fangs. All this just to avoid running into a sign. If only I hadn't taken Jovi's cry so seriously, I'd still be standing on two feet with my arms full of tapes.

A chalkboard sign blocked half of the sidewalk, announcing discount dog grooming for the holiday. *Get Fido ready for the family reunion!* Hollow eyes of a crudely drawn pirate skull stared back at me from beneath the words.

I snuffled, half-sneezing and half-barking, and then gathered my clothes in my mouth before a passerby had time to see my granny panties. At least my fur kept me warmer than this old sweater and the kids happily carried the tapes.

When we arrived at the rink, I slipped past the skate rental counter to the back corner where "Restrooms" was splashed across the wall in neon paint. The turquoise, pink, and purple matched the sporadic swirls decorating the dark blue floor. The psychedelic carpet covered every inch of the floor except the skating rink's maple hardwood and the tile in the bathrooms and diner section.

Inside a stall, I took a deep breath and gathered enough energy to shift back to human form and slip into my clothes. Jovi waited by the restrooms, hands full of VHS tapes as an excuse to avoid roller skating. When I relieved him of the videos, he found a quiet booth in the corner of the diner and pulled out the book he'd borrowed from the library for the third time: *Matilda*.

I scanned the busy rink for my other pups, spotting Stevie in the center as she pushed Sir Crabby and Squeaks around in each of her skates. Dio and Halen zipped in and out of skaters in a never-ending race to prove themselves the fastest. The laughter and smiles warmed my heart.

I picked my way through the crowded diner until I spotted the new roller rink owner. Crow's midnight-black curls caught my eye, and a grin spread across half of his face. He didn't smile with his whole mouth, but the scar cutting through his cheek almost extended the grin for him. Though he wasn't a ghost, he looked almost as pale, and a chill sloughed off of him. If he hadn't already told me he was a human, I'd believe he was one of the rarer warlocks with seasonal magic—particularly winter. Of course, if he were a skilled warlock, we wouldn't have to wait for Professor Rowena to cast the protection spell.

"Hey, it's Noema the wolf," he said as he leaned against the skate rental counter and gestured to the videotapes in my arms. "Have you come to fulfill our deal?"

It sounded like an illegal exchange the way the words slipped off his tongue. I didn't know him well, but I intended to change that because his smooth jokes both set me at ease and sent my heart skipping.

Like several other newcomers, Crow had taken advantage of the low housing market after the town's only real estate agent was arrested for murder.

"Crow the..." I glanced around at the skates hanging behind his head. "The Roller Rink Owner, I come bearing gifts." I played along with his curious behavior and secretly transferred the goods into his possession. "This should keep the riff raff happy."

Crow snorted and mumbled. "In my business, nobody is happy." *In...roller skating?* I kept the thought to myself and caught a whiff of fish—the smell of guilt. Odd. Maybe the diner had decided to serve Halibut. He raised his voice and his dark eyes met mine. "The college kids that are stuck in town have taken to studying here late at night. They've been complaining that they're sick of watching the news. Especially that warlock kid. He comes in and gets drunk and then whines to my employees about the boring crap on TV. Apparently, he's got some kind of talent with electrical magic, and one time he rewired all our TVs to only play MTV."

"Music Television? That's not so bad."

He clucked his tongue. "Yeah, try telling that to fifty elementary school moms when inappropriate songs come on during their six-year-old's birthday party."

"Sounds like a pain in the rear," I said and nodded toward the tapes. "Hopefully the comedies will keep him happy."

He smirked, and I couldn't help but admire his sharp jawline and the way his eyes lit up with mischief. "Ah, but I thought you had a more manipulative plan than merely keeping my customers happy."

My cheeks flushed hot. Whether it was from his wink or the suggestion that my sneaky business proposition was illicit, I couldn't tell. I shrugged, and the oversized sweater nearly slipped off my shoulder. I tugged it into place, and my gaze trailed to a television mounted on the wall in the diner. "I suppose after they watch the movies here, they might want to rent the sequels from me. But who am I to deny Bewitcher's Beach a little entertainment? Especially during this storm."

Crow laughed. "I'm all for entertainment. Which movies do you recommend?"

A blush burned from my cheeks all the way to my temples as we talked, and his questions focused on getting to know me. Werewolves always run hot, but it was even more obvious against Crow's cool demeanor. Clawed fingers landed on my shoulder, and Crow's gaze shifted behind me.

"As a romantic, I hate to interrupt this little tryst," Mae said. The elderly half-dragon pulled her hand back and slapped her palm against her chest. Her long fingernails snagged on her fuzzy pink sweater. The smell of ammonia from her worried emotions rose around me, tickling my nose. Like all half-dragons, she resembled a human except for the shimmer of scales beneath her skin, claw-like fingernails, and faint red eyes. "But your poor little baby girl is crying." She pointed across the roller rink.

Stevie sat in the center of the skating floor with her head in her hands. Her bony shoulders shook with sobs, and her torso expanded and shrank with rapid breaths.

I immediately abandoned the conversation and loped across the rink, my sneakers sliding and slipping on the slick, waxy floor. Once I dodged skaters and clumsily made my way to the center, I dropped to my knees and wrapped my arms around my daughter. "What happened?" The wet earth aroma of sadness accompanied the tears in her shimmering eyes.

She sucked in a quivering breath. "Jovi and I were skating together, but I told him to go away. He said we don't get to celebrate the holidays because we don't have any family." Another shuddering breath forced her rambling to pause. "And–and he said that everybody else will have reunions but we don't get *anything*. I wanted a big celebration with pudding and cake too!"

My heart cracked because she wasn't wrong. We were our only family, no reunions and no cousins, but that didn't mean we couldn't throw a party. A glimmer of hope and an idea kept my tears at bay. "Actually, Stevie, celebrating the holiday with Hattie and our other friends will just make us part of the Bewitcher's Beach family. And of course there will be a big celebration; even if we're not meeting with family, we can bake a cake and decorate Mockbuster."

She wiped her nose and looked up at me with big doe eyes. The disco ball above us caught the shine of wetness on her cheeks. They crinkled with the little smile that spread across her face. "Really?"

"Really." As the lemon-lime fizz of happiness swirled in the air around us, I gave her a squeeze. I stood and scoped the rink for the culprit, discovering Jovi had returned to a booth in the diner with his nose inside a book. I marched across the rink and into the diner, plopping down in the seat opposite him and tapping my fingers on the table until he lowered the book. The smell of fish—guilt—wafted from him, and he curled his lips inward. "What do you have to say for yourself?"

"The truth," he barked as he slumped back into the vinyl bench. "I know you think the holiday will make us officially Bewitched or whatever, but nobody here is our real family."

So much for happiness. The rainy aroma returned, stronger this time as it emanated from both of us.

Mae, in her endless desire for drama, sidled up to our table and slid into the booth beside me with two cups of tea. The grandmotherly half-dragon gave Jovi an apologetic look and slipped him a dollar for game tokens before sliding her second teacup to me.

Despite the little gift, Jovi still reeked of disappointment. I reached across the table and laid my hand on his wrist. "I know it's not the same as relatives, but friends are a type of family." Even as I said it, the swell in my throat squeezed the words. I wanted to believe it as much as I wanted to convince him.

He snuffed. "Too bad you weren't born a werewolf like us, then you wouldn't have forgotten your family." The truth stung. Once I'd turned, I couldn't remember anybody or anything from life before, like all bitten werewolves.

I suppressed a growl of frustration and reminded myself my son only wanted the same thing that I did: family.

"It doesn't matter anyway," he huffed. He dropped the book onto the table and crossed his arms. "I heard my friend's mom say the holidays are getting canceled."

Tingles spread over my skin, and I folded my ears back. "What?"

"Well he's not wrong," Mae said, patting Jovi's shoulder in her grandmotherly way. "Didn't you hear? Barney, Mayor Fitz, and even Sheriff Sett are meeting right now to discuss canceling the Ghost Pirate Moon invitation. The sheriff said it's just too dangerous since some of the pirates' spirits may have become poltergeists. And we all know poltergeists like to break stuff and throw things at us living folks. It's always a risk with that many spirits visiting at once, but now, people could get seriously hurt if they encounter an angry spirit."

A knot tightened in my chest.

Jovi saw Mae's distraction as an opportunity to slip away without a lecture. He hopped out of the other side of the booth and hurried to the rink.

"Plus, it's too dangerous after the fall festival's murder, and..." Mae leaned in, drawing us closer together with her voice dropping to a conspiratorial whisper. "Since the protection spell is gone, this cancellation is only the beginning. They're going to end every single holiday if they get their way, and they'll definitely try to sway our votes at the town forum. If you ask me, they're just a bunch of weenies. Life is always a risk!"

If only Madam Rowena could get here to weave the spell, Bewitcher's Beach would be safe enough for holiday celebrations...for families to gather. I wished anyone with a witch in their bloodline could cast the protection spell, but those with traces of spellwork magic weren't powerful enough to wield intention spells, only minor magic like lighting a candle, summoning across short distances, or healing a sour stomach.

The warlock Crow had mentioned certainly wielded powerful magic if he'd come from Shadowvale University. Could he recreate the protection spell?

My heart flipped, beating erratically as an idea formed, and I glanced across the diner at Crow, who was chatting with Mae's husband. When he caught my eye, he bid Wallace goodbye and walked over to the table. Mae—always ready to gossip—filled him in on our conversation.

I smiled at the thought of asking the young warlock to give the new spell a try. For the holiday, for my kids, and for all Bewitched. "I know how to change Sett and Mayor Fitz's minds."

Mae gasped, more dramatically than the situation called for. As usual. "Then we'd better get you to that meeting."

"Not me." I nodded at Crow. "They need to meet the warlock from Shadowvale and see *The Book of Prophecies* for themselves. I've read the protection spell a million times now, and even though I'm not a witch, I swear it's simpler than a lot of the other spells in the book. I bet he could pull it off."

Crow nodded as he leaned against the top of the booth with one elbow and crossed his feet out in front of him. "You're talking about Fate Kalabar? Do you really want to risk a college kid trying the spell?"

I nodded, exchanging a smirk with him. No way would I let them cancel the biggest family event of the year.

My gaze shifted to the rink, where Jovi had finally joined his brothers and sister. The kids laughed, shoved one another, and skated in circles. The people of Bewitcher's Beach were the only family they'd ever had.

"Yes, because that spell belongs here. It's part of our *home*."

CHAPTER 2
CLUELESS

WHILE MAE SETTLED into a booth to keep an eye on my pups, I shoved through Roller Shakes's double doors. I marched outside, fueled by the determination of a mama bear ready to protect the holiday that her cubs wanted to celebrate.

The sky roared. Thunder announced its booming arrival, and rain fell in forceful sheets, blurring my view of the brick library across town.

The storm was another reminder that our town had been unfairly stripped of the spell that protected Bewitcher's Beach. The woven magic had been an invisible blanket that made it impossible for people to hurt one another, stopping them in their tracks, and—like the once mysteriously endless breeze— the spell whirled the attacker away from their target and swept all nefarious intentions away just as it did with dangerous weather.

Once I had the grimoire in my hands, I'd track down the only warlock in town and request Fate's aid with the magic of protection.

I cut through the park at the center of town, where the grass squashed beneath my feet. The field sagged from the weight of the pelting rain, and the suction of the soaked soil pulled in a puckering squelch with every step. By the time I reached the other side of town, the downpour mixed with the sound of the crashing waves.

Flickering silver and red lights were strung across the library's windows, and a black wreath with tiny wire ships hung at the center of the door. The wind violently whipped a black flag with a skull and crossbones about. The black fabric ripped right off the pole and flew away, dancing in the storm for a moment before the heavy rain pinned it to the cobblestone. The flag lay lifeless only a few steps away from my soaked sneakers.

I frowned at the ominous sight and shook off the excess water as if I were in my wolf form. It didn't work as well while I was human, but at least the water clinging to my eyelashes blinked away. It was then I saw the smashed glass on the window to the right.

My breath hitched at the sight of the damage.

The librarian scowled at me from the inside, where she stood several steps away from the window to keep dry. The red-headed woman wore lensless glasses with plastic knobs that jutted from the brown frames in the shape of a miniature ship's helm, partially shrouding her one green eye and one red eye from her distant dragon ancestry. She pulled her gaze from me to stare at the torn flag on the ground. Her crimson eye and the slight shimmer to her skin were the only evidence that she had dragon blood somewhere in her human ancestry.

"Hi Judy," I said with the most apologetic smile I could muster. It wasn't my fault the storm had arrived to ruin the holidays, all our decorations, and, apparently, the library's window. I stepped up to the door and pushed through, now viewing the damage from the inside.

Judy sighed but did not give me the respect of her attention, instead only shaking her head at the shards of glass that littered the floor. The broken pieces were scattered over the library's odd rugs that overlapped one another. Glittering glass caught the soft glow of the yellow bulbs in the dangling lights above.

"Did the wind do this?" I asked.

Judy huffed and spun around. "Don't be naive, Noema Wolf; this is the work of a vicious criminal." Her fists curled at her sides so tightly that the skin of her knuckles strained white. "If I could just get my hands on them, I'd show them two can play this destruction game."

What would someone break into the library for? I scanned the room of tall shelves, round tables, and a seemingly endless supply of well-loved books. The library looked intact everywhere except the window and the water damage to the books on the small shelf beside it. Judy's sharp fingernail traced the spine of a destroyed copy of *The Hardy Boys: Hunting for Hidden Gold*. A trail of thin smoke emitted from her petite nose. As a partial dragon, Judy treated the books like her own gold, her own hoard, and she guarded them with her life. Whoever had caused the ruin of this shelf of classic mysteries would become the focus of her fiery wrath, and I didn't envy them one bit. Time to get the *Book of Prophecies* and get out before she took her temper out on me. "What else did they ruin?"

"You mean other than my life? This library is everything to me. Anyway, I don't know. I've only just arrived for the day." The smoky scent of her anger mixed with a distinct fishy odor that only came from...guilt. Odd. What did Judy have to feel guilty for? The oily, rancid fish mixed with the smell of old books, and my stomach turned. "I came to take my pirate decorations inside before the storm destroyed them. Thanks to this mess, I've gotten nothing done." It dawned on me that Judy didn't actually live at the library the way my little family made our home above Mockbuster. She'd always been here, a constant like the thousands of books crammed—organized, but crammed—into this quaint brick building. After a huff, Judy turned and painted on a neutral expression as she adjusted the odd glasses that perched on the bridge of her nose and curled her lips into the politest smile. "What can I help you find?"

My stomach churned, unsettled at the sight of her masked temper. But she was trying her hardest to do her job in an upsetting situation, and that was a feeling I knew all too well after a murder derailed my video shop with rumors. When I cleared my throat and requested the grimoire, Judy quickly jumped into action, and the tension eased as she hurried to retrieve it.

Unlike the rest of the books, *The Book of Prophecies* was stored behind the librarian's desk on a shelf full of curious and precious trinkets. A fragile skull and a tattered copy of *Pirate History Off the Californian Coast* decorated the specialized shelf for the coming holiday alongside rare books. Despite the gorgeous crystal ball on the bottom shelf and the framed strip of a treasure map, my gaze remained glued to the book of spells at the very top.

The Book of Prophecies called to me. After it'd been lost for a decade, hidden in a secret hollow in the library's back shelves and covered in shadow and dust, I'd sensed it.

Two months ago, I'd found it.

Now I knew what pulled me to the prophecies—a peculiar and promising scent.

As the librarian's bony fingers gripped the spine, the strange smell flooded my nose. A smell I recognized but couldn't describe. A smell that calmed my pounding heart and reminded me of love and hugs and homemade meals.

Of course, the last homemade meal I'd smelled was from

Sett. He'd dropped off a tupperware container of fettuccine Alfredo at Mockbuster Video Rental with the hopes that I'd waive his late fee for *Jurassic Park*. *Sett and his stupid idea to ruin the biggest family reunion*...my hackles raised at the reminder.

A little growl escaped me until Judy blinked up at me through the lensless glasses and shook her head.

After she put the book down, she whipped out a box of cleaning supplies. The box fell from her hands and slammed against the desk with a thud right on top of my fingers before I could reach for the book. Apparently, her temper was already rearing its ugly head, and I was the only target around for her anger to focus on.

"Oops." She shrugged, and the hard line of her mouth didn't waver as she tucked locks of fiery red hair behind her ears. Half a dozen shimmering, dangling earrings hung from holes in her lobes all the way up to the tip. Irritation wafted from her with a car exhaust's woody petroleum. If her purposeful slip of the hand didn't clue me in on her frustration, the hint of gasoline confirmed it.

The tension melted as I reached for the book and peace washed over me. I cupped the spine in my palm and fanned through the pages, absorbing the smells. Christmas morning cinnamon bread. Rose perfume. Wool yarn. *Mmm.*

Warmth swelled within me, firing up my already-toasty wolf fever.

The book that'd captured my heart's attention was going to save the Ghost Pirate Moon celebration and bring joy to hundreds of families in Bewitcher's Beach. Giddiness returned, fluttering in my chest like a pixie's wings.

I paused to soak in the whiff of pot roast on a page with a recipe before thumbing ahead to an empty spot in the grimoire's spine. The edges were frayed where an entire section was missing. My heartbeat stumbled once, twice, and then spluttered into an irregular rhythm.

The spell was gone.

Where handwritten notes were once scrawled across the pages, only shredded paper remained in the binding, and the hope I carried high in my heart dropped like the anchor of a pirate ship.

CHAPTER 3
FRIGHT CLUB

"NO," I breathed. "No, no, no!"

I flipped through the book again to be sure I'd looked in the correct spot. The protection spell was definitely gone. It had been ripped right from the binding, torn haphazardly from its original home.

Air was sucked from my lungs, and I doubled over, dropping the book open on the desk with my hands splayed out on either side. I tried to catch my breath as I stared at the torn pages.

"How could this happen?" I glanced at the shattered window and the sheets of rain dumping on the other side.

I tore my eyes from the missing pages and looked up to see Judy adjust her glasses as if they'd help her better scrutinize the ruined book. The crook of her peaked, pencil-lined brow matched the mingled scents of confusion and regret. She smelled of pineapple pizza on burnt toast until smoky anger took over.

"Why am I not surprised?" The hair she'd tucked back fell into her face as she bent over the desk and flipped the book around. Twisting her neck, Judy narrowed her gaze at the broken window and the ruined shelf of books beneath. "Another destroyed book to add to the list of offenses. This intruder may as well have ripped off my arm." Her voice caught, and her hands curled into fists until she could hold it back no longer. The odor of smoke filled the space between us, squeezing a cough from my chest as I watched her freckled face turn red, eyes still fixed on the damage. Judy slammed her knuckles against the desk and released a string of curses I knew were stolen from classic literature thanks to Jovi's bookworm tendencies.

"You're sure the intruder did this?"

She scoffed. "Well I certainly wouldn't allow a book to be ripped while under my watch, and I know this grimoire never left the library. So it must have happened with the break-in."

My mind went into overdrive, trying to make sense of the situation. If someone broke in to steal the spell, they had to know where to find it first. In a library full of magical books and minor spells, that was no easy task. "Who borrowed it last?" I stabbed the open page, my finger landing on a sketch of the Kraken in black ink.

Frazzled but focused, Judy tore the glasses from her face and tossed them on the desktop before stooping to retrieve her record box. The old-fashioned librarian refused to update to a computer system, having once called mine an "abomination to natural organization." She'd never returned to Mockbuster after that and hadn't so much as touched a movie during her one-time visit, much less rented one.

Gently, deftly, she flicked through the hundreds of note-cards arranged alphabetically and then plucked from behind the "P" card.

"It was Fate Kalabar." The exact college kid I wanted to track down.

My hammering heart slowed. Maybe Fate already had it;

maybe he was one step ahead of me and was working on casting it. Or maybe he didn't, and I was two steps behind on the plan. The thought left a sour taste on my tongue. "We need this spell. If we can't cast it, the Ghost Pirate Moon will be canceled."

Judy's throat bobbed in a hard swallow, and she absently thumbed a dangling earring with her free hand. The green jewels on the parrot charm clinked against gold rings on her fingers. "I assume a cancellation will be discussed at the town forum? I wait every decade to talk with my Great Aunt Judith. She'd want me to vote for the holiday so we may visit with one another, as we do every ten years..." Her voice faded, and she focused on me again, frowning. "Anyway, what do you care? You'll probably get more business as people drown their sorrows in mind-melting movies—"

"I'll fix this." I said, interrupting her rant before I slipped into disappointment and frustration along with her. "I can bring this to Fate and have him put the spell back when he's done." With the grimoire in my hands, I turned toward the door and took a step.

"That book isn't supposed to leave the library." She snapped. "Noema, stop!"

The door slammed shut behind me, cutting off another list of classic literature curses. I wasn't supposed to take the book, sure, but I wasn't supposed to do a lot of things I'd done in the last few months. Like I wasn't supposed to involve myself in murder investigations, I wasn't supposed to date again, and I wasn't supposed to watch the next episode of any soap opera without Mae.

But family *was* supposed to be together for a holiday, and this book would make that possible for many Bewitched citizens. Library's rules or not, I wanted the book in my arms since it smelled of home and the family I dreamed of. I hugged it to my chest even as a thought nagged me. If the protection spell was gone, where had the scent that reminded me of family and love come from? I'd assumed the comfort of protection was what drew me to it. Like a mother's hug or a father holding his child's hand as they crossed the street. Because I wanted to meet my family so badly, I thought the smell drew me to it.

The briny breeze that tangled through my curls snapped my attention to the present.

The rain had slowed for a moment, inviting in a bone-chilling wind that whipped the waves of hair from my face. I power-walked against the current, using the strength of my thick thighs to speed up. Walking on two legs was far slower than bolting on four paws, but there was no way I would risk hurting the book more to shift into my wolf form. On all fours, I'd have to carry it between my sharp teeth.

The stone path to the beach called to my soul. The wild werewolf within begged to take a run in the sand. A run would burn off the tension from the librarian, rid myself of the memory of the pain in Stevie's voice, and shake thoughts of disappointment if my plan didn't work. But the shore, the lapping waves, and salty mist would only taunt me, reminding me of the pirate spirits lost at sea. Without the invitation—the message of the backward rotation from the lighthouse's beam—they'd never find their way to shore, where living beings kept them sane and relatives rejoiced at the reunion.

I took a sharp right from the path and away from the ocean. When a figure caught my eye, I doubled back and squinted. A tall man in a duster marched across the sand several yards away.

"Crow?"

But when the man vanished behind the gray stones that mottled the lighthouse's cylindrical base, I moved on, assuming it was the vampire who worked nights tending the lighthouse.

The closer I drew to the houses on the beach, the harder

my heart rapped against my ribcage. I passed a haunted house where the spirit of a murdered man resided. Cliff Conflick's ghost co-existed alongside Gemma, Sett's *friend*—the town's new cop who'd purchased the home as soon as she moved into town. A light winked out in the front window, drawing my attention to the flickering curtain as the ghost vanished from view.

Hugging the book to my chest, I jogged ahead, leaving the haunted house in my wake. I hurried to the end of the street where the Kalabar family beach house towered over the more modest homes. It was one of the largest and most expensive houses in town. According to Mae, the family of wealthy witches and warlocks paid a very pretty penny for it just to vacation here each summer.

Their college son clearly didn't care about the state of this home from the outside since he'd let the grass become over-grown and left beer cans littering the front yard. Hopefully his affinity for parties and alcohol didn't inhibit his ability with spells and magic.

I picked through the tall weeds to the front door. Other than the crashing, distant waves beyond the house and an occasional owl's hoot, the street was dead quiet. My heaving breaths broke the silence, exposing how embarrassingly out-of-shape my human form had become. Mom life didn't leave a lot of moments for step aerobics.

After carefully shifting the book beneath my left arm, I raised my fist to the door and knocked. Hinges moaned as the door creaked open. Either I'd banged too forcefully or the wind had switched directions, and by the looks of the door, it'd been through a beating. The brassy knob was scratched at the keyhole, and the bottom right corner of the wood was dented, like it'd been met with the toe of a boot one too many times.

"Fate?" I coughed to clear my throat. "Mr. Kalabar?"

No response.

Antsy now, my fingers tightened around the book's spine, and I squeezed it closer into my ribs.

The breeze picked up again, whipping hair into my eyes and mouth and carrying with it the heavy, horrible scent of must and decay—an odor that was far stronger than a withering emotion.

My stomach turned like a rolling wave, crashing and tucking back in on itself. I held my breath, pursing my lips tightly as I tapped the door.

Creaking, it opened under the weight of my hand, and I stepped over the threshold. I opened my mouth to call out his name, but my voice died in my throat. A curdling smell beckoned me with curiosity into the grand entryway that was littered with more crushed beer cans, clothes strewn about, an open toolkit on the glittering tile floor, and a discarded backpack with notebooks falling from the unzipped flap. Did this frat boy's family know about the way he treated their vacation home? Likely not, or else they'd have hired a cleaner.

"Fate?" My voice cracked in a weak whisper. As I followed the smell, I passed a large mudroom and laundry area where beachgoers could shake off sandy clothes and immediately drop them into a basket or the washing machine. Fate had trashed that room too, leaving piles of dirty laundry, and based on the sour smell, he had yet to wash them.

After a sneeze, my nose cleared enough to follow the curdling scent again. It led me into a large study where giant oak bookcases lined the walls. A matching dark wooden desk was pushed against the shelves along with the maroon leather chairs. My gaze fell to the center of the room, where it seemed a mad scientist had redecorated with a plastic table, wires, and cluttered piles of paper.

At the sight of the mad scientist himself, a vise gripped my heart

Right in the middle of the study lay his body.

In a haze, I floated over to Fate with the hope that I'd hear his faint breath or see the reassuring rise and fall of his chest. Instead, the warlock's blank eyes stared lifelessly at the ceiling, and the book fell from my hand with a sickening thud against the floorboards. *The Book of Prophecies* fell open where the pages were missing right in the crook of Fate's rigid blue-and-purple-mottled arm.

And at the sight of his unseeing eyes, I screamed.

CHAPTER 4
SCREAM

THE HOWL from my churning belly came to a sudden halt. I slapped my hand to my chest, trying to calm my heaving breaths. The night had only gotten worse with the missing spell and a dead body. So much worse.

I clamped my jaw shut and sucked in a gasp through my nose. Bad idea. The smell of death and Fate's lingering scent of fear burned. I gagged and pinched my nose but not before another lingering odor mixed with the victim's stench of ammonia.

Smoke. Distinctly different from the nauseating scent of burnt plastic brought on by the deadly wire. Was I smelling anger? Could it be my own frustration deep down that our only hope for the protection spell was now dead? No. I was worried, startled, and sad for the young warlock who'd lost his life. Not angry.

But I'd never smelled anger near a dead body before, not even at the crime scene a few weeks back.

Pull yourself together, Noema. You don't know what you're smelling.

As soon as my pulse eased into a normal rhythm, I scanned the scene.

Colorful spines of hardcover books stood out in a room full of dark oak furniture and floorboards. Everything was the epitome of sophistication from the expensive fountain pen on the massive desk to the ornate iron floor lamp that almost matched the black posts along the cobblestone streets.

And then there was Fate's redecoration. Or rather, his science project. Tangled electrical wires were strewn across the little vinyl tabletop, piled upon one another in twists and spirals. Long , colorful, arm-like cords hung over the edge but didn't reach the floor. Amongst the mess, a curious pattern wove through the wires with black being the most dominant. Red, blue, and yellow cables were braided around one another, but the bright plastic protection didn't cover most of the electrical wire.

Exposed raw wiring buzzed with power. Power coming straight from the magic-infused wires. I took a step back from the table, knowing I needed to get out of here before I tripped over my own two feet and wound up electrocuted.

One wrong move and then the wire would be the only live thing in this room. Again.

"What happened to you?" I whispered, voice squeaking and rough with emotion for the poor young man. "Did you trip and fall into a science experiment gone wrong?" Even as I said it, I knew it wasn't likely. Despite the mess in the rest of the house, the floor in this room was clean. There were no cords or papers or crumpled clothes on the ground, only flat, even floorboards. And if Crow had been right, this college kid was no slouch when it came to electrical magic and wiring.

I avoided Fate's lifeless eyes while I glanced over his body, noting the redness and abrasions around his wrists and the burn on his hand that hinted at electrocution. Tiny crescent marks dimpled his wrists as if someone had grabbed him hard enough to dig their fingernails into his flesh. Bile burned at the back of my throat. The bitter taste jolted me.

The police needed to be notified immediately.

I straightened and scanned the study for a phone. The cream landline was buried beneath wires and plugged into a power strip with scorch marks from too much electrical magic. As soon as I reached for it, I yanked my hand back. One touch and I could be barbeque wolf meat. Even the spiral plastic cord was tangled in the wires as if hooked together purposefully.

If only I'd bought that cell phone I had my eye on, I'd be able to alert Sett of the situation. I'd have to ask to borrow someone else's phone. I hurried through the house and ducked out the door.

Outside, I spotted another house a half mile down the road, one I knew belonged to a kind shifter family, but it appeared nobody was home. Likely, the parents had taken their home-schooled son, Noodle, to the rink for social time with the other kids as they often did on busy nights at Roller Shakes.

I set my sights on the next house in the neighborhood and tucked *The Book of Prophecies* tighter into my torso. There the loose sweater buried the grimoire in fabric that would protect it in case of sudden rainfall. Tall oleander bushes lined the opposite end of the street, giving the beachfront homes privacy from the library and the kid-packed neighborhood beyond. The thick brush cast long shadows over the sandy road. Another shadow crossed over me, but I ignored the night's bats and owls flying overhead. I marched alongside the bushes, heading for the next house when a figure emerged from the shadows and almost collided with me.

A gasp escaped me, and the stranger's creased face

mirrored my surprise. The stunning, brown-skinned woman looked up at me with shining dark eyes filled with worry and shadowed by the brim of her pointed pink hat. She wore a pink sweater under her stone-washed overalls that matched her witch hat. The hat's black rim pulled the outfit together, coordinating with the black straps of the backpack that was slung over her shoulders. She leaned a knotted wooden broomstick against her hip and removed her hat, revealing two full buns of brown hair.

"I'm sorry," she said. "Did my broom hit you? I'm terrible with landings and always dizzy when I try to walk after." Her words tumbled over one another, spilling out faster than I could focus. "This awful wind has made it impossible for me to fly any farther than a couple of blocks before it tries to kill me. I can't get my course straight when I'm blown all around. You know? So if my broom bumped you, I'm seriously sorry." It took me an extra moment to straighten my thoughts as she rambled.

It suddenly made sense—I didn't see her on the street because she was above me.

"Uh, no. You didn't hit me," I said, gathering myself before my imagination ran away with dreams of this new witch casting the protection spell. It felt inappropriate to hope for her help so soon after the warlock's disturbing death.

"Phew!" She mocked the action of wiping sweat away from her forehead, and her lips split into a dazzling grin as she laughed. "This wouldn't be the first time I've crash landed into an innocent person. Though I have to admit, being clumsy isn't all that bad, you know? I'm just waiting for the day I bump into my soulmate and our hands touch as he helps me pick up my homework."

I bit back a smile, another inappropriate behavior in light of Fate's circumstances. "Like in romance movies?"

The witch straightened and the broom fell to the sandy

street. "Yes! This girl gets it," she said as she pointed her thumb at me.

As much as I wanted to chat romcoms and clumsiness with this friendly newcomer—and as the resident movie buff, I could talk about it all night—dread crept into my gut at the memory of my mission. Find a phone and get the police. "Do you have a pager or a cell phone by any chance? It's an emergency."

She nodded and stuffed her free hand into the overall's side pocket, which tugged at her shirt, the collar dipping and revealing an inky mark above her heart. The tattoo-like mark's jagged shape resembled Sett's wings, spread like open hands with spiky fingers reaching down. "Is everything okay?" she asked, voice light and cheerful but with an appropriate touch of concern.

"Not exactly."

After a moment, she pulled out a crystal charm bracelet and a tiny corked potion bottle. Both common for any witch to carry. She shoved the items into her other pocket and finally produced a small black communication device. "Number?"

"The police," I said around the feel of a cotton ball in my dry mouth. "For 401 Beach Street."

Her mouth fell open as she sucked in a sharp breath and froze.

"Fate's house?" Her voice was a whisper, and her gaze shifted to the mansion behind me as the creases deepened. She looked only to be in her early twenties, too young for so much worry. Her brows lifted but she finally nodded and dialed the emergency line. While she called the police station, I held my breath. "Hi. I'm calling about an emergency at 401 Beach Street." After a pause, she thanked them and pressed a button to end the call. I opened my mouth to express my gratitude but she spoke before I could get a word out. "Excuse me." The witch darted around me, breaking into a light jog toward Fate's house. She left ammonia, the pungent stench of fear, lingering in her wake.

I hurried after her and hoped to stop her before she had to see the harsh sight of Fate's lifeless gaze. But the witch was already inside and frozen at the threshold of the study with her broom tucked beneath her arm. She was a reflection of me only moments before with the *Book of Prophecies* under the crook of my elbow.

"No," she sobbed, doubling forward as if sick to her stomach. "No, no, no. You tried to spell without me?" Her voice was a shriek now as her tears dripped on the floor around the body.

"Were you friends with Fate?"

She spun around, startled as if she'd entirely forgotten me or thought I'd remained outside. "Friends? I—uh..." The worry returned with the downward curve of her mouth and tears in her eyes that quickly dried. "Nope, definitely not."

With that, she dipped around me. She scurried out the front door before she swung her leg over the broom and took flight, leaving me in a stupor with my mouth hanging open. Before I could muster a response or determine the scent of her mixed emotions, she disappeared into the shadows.

I floated to the door in a daze and scanned the dark clouds for any sign of the friendly witch. Who was she to Fate? Only the sky rippled in response to my thoughts. The storm belched another warning that it was ready to dump buckets of rain over Bewitcher's Beach.

I only hoped the frazzled young witch would be safe flying in the storm. Though the roiling clouds blocked any sight of the woman and her broom, I got lost in the search as I squinted for any sign of her.

"What is it, Wolf? Never seen a storm before?" A woman laughed.

I blinked at the sight of Gemma, Sett's old girlfriend, old

friend, old *partner* in fighting crime before he became the sheriff of Bewitcher's Beach. Clear, ocean blue eyes rolled into the back of her head before her gaze shifted beyond me. Smooth gel and a simple black elastic kept her blonde hair pulled into a tight ponytail that wiggled when she walked. She picked through the weeds, marching with determination as she shouldered past me and through the doorway, carefully stepping over the raised threshold.

How long had I been standing in a daze and staring at the sky? It seemed only a minute or two had passed, and Gemma was suddenly here. "No, there was a witch," I said. She laughed, a loud raspy sound, and I waited for it to end before I spoke again "Where's Sett?"

"*Sheriff* Lawrence is on his way," she said, unhurried in her casual tone. "Now, where's the victim?" She gathered her ponytail in one hand, twisted, and with her other hand tucked it at the back of her head. Once the black jaws of a claw clip secured the hair in place, she kicked a lumpy sweatshirt out of the way with the toe of her boot.

I led Gemma through the maze of the messy entryway and into the study where Fate had been abandoned.

With a sigh, she hooked her thumbs through her belt loops. She shook her head at the body by her feet. "Poor sap must have had a death wish playing with this much raw wire. I've seen pyromaniacs blow themselves up like this. Witches and warlocks included." Another sigh, harsher and followed by pursed lips. Finally, she snapped blue latex gloves onto her hands and crouched over Fate. "Of course, delinquents aren't the only ones who take these little side hobbies too far." Her gaze ticked up, landing on me like a crashing wave. "You're the werewolf who sniffed out the murderer last month, right?"

At the prickled tone of her voice, my hackles raised in mild defense.

"Uh, yeah, that's me." I'd only spoken with Gemma once since she moved in. Though they were friends, she never accompanied Sett on his visits to Mockbuster. Instead, she kept to the station where she'd covered Mayor Fitz's previous duties as a volunteer police officer.

"We professionals have got it from here." Her voice cut through my thoughts, and she waved her hand as if to shoo me away. "You can leave."

The odor of gasoline mixed with hints of sandalwood. The smells radiated from her as she glared at me over the dead body. She was both angry and confident, the latter likely regarding her skill with crime scenes.

"I–" I clamped my jaw shut. She was right, I should leave. The grimoire's pages weren't here that I could see, and I needed to find out where they'd ended up if the warlock didn't have them.

Despite her dismissal, I wanted to help, given the ease with which I could sniff out guilty suspects. But involving myself in another investigation so soon after the murder in front of Mockbuster would only dig up weeks-old gossip.

The people of Bewitcher's Beach were superstitious, if not a little spooked after the protection spell was first confirmed as the source of their decades of safety and then subsequently stripped away.

They were spooked. I was spooked. Gemma the cop was *not* spooked.

She practically glowed, thriving as she set to work taking notes on a yellow legal pad and carefully plucking plastic wire to peer underneath it. Goosebumps crawled up my arms as I watched her casually flick and prod and touch the crime scene as if she was familiar with it. How had she arrived so quickly when the witch only just made the call? A call which mentioned nothing about a death... *Where's the victim?* I supposed a crime was assumed when one requested police help. And where there was crime, no matter the type, there was usually a victim.

Still, Gemma's sudden arrival and the way she poked at the body unsettled me. Sett was always careful and caring, sensitive and protective at any crime scene, which was nothing like the behavior of this cop he'd once dated.

In fact, it was impossible to picture the two of them together with her dismissive demeanor and his protective tendencies. Sure he was made of stone, but she was the one with a heart of rock. Certainly not someone Sett could find attractive...

Was I jealous of Gemma? A strange scent emanated from the twist in my gut, confirming it. I shook my head at the crazy speculation that she was somehow the cause of Fate's...fate. She had no motive.

I should have hurried home before the next rainfall, but I couldn't bring myself to move. Something about the weaving of the wires nagged at my memory, reminding me what I'd read in *The Book of Prophecies*. I squeezed my eyes shut and tried to remember the protection spell, the way the witch had explained the braided tendrils of magic, and the comparison of raw power to soft yarn as she'd threaded magic around a crochet hook and created a massive, invisible force—like a blanket over Bewitcher's Beach. A blanket that blocked out any possibility that a supernatural creature could be attacked. Could wires and cords work the same way as yarn?

BEFORE I KNEW IT, Sett, the coroner, and Mayor Fitz —still involving himself as a volunteer officer when it interested him— swarmed the study. Sett drilled me with the usual questions. I explained my reason for being here, how I found Fate, and that I'd met a witch who'd called for help.

The coroner confirmed my suspicions. Cause of death was very likely electrocution by Fate's own wiring project. A wiring project with a pattern...

The same pattern as the protection spell.

My heart thumped erratically as I flipped the book open to the missing pages and tried to imagine what I'd seen when I first had access to the grimoire.

Sett cupped my elbow with his rough hand, cooling my burning wolf's fever with his gentle touch. "Are you all right, Noema? You're looking a little...queasy?"

I blinked and shook my head, though he wasn't wrong. A swell of dizziness had me leaning into his hold for a moment. "I'm upset about the book. It looks like Fate took the protection spell and now it could be lost. It had the answers to keeping our tradition"—my eyes dropped to Fate's face just before the coroner zipped the black body bag over his head—"alive. If I'm being honest, I'm sad for him *and* the holiday. I'd hoped he could recreate the protection spell in time to stop you and Mayor Fitz from canceling the celebration."

"You're not the only one against the idea, but it's for the best. There could be poltergeists aboard that ship, and we don't want them hurting residents. We'll be voting on it tomorrow night, and I believe the town will listen to reason."

I snorted. "Yeah, and now with another murderer—"

"Murderer?" Sett's brow wrinkled and his slate eyes turned stony, intense as he glared at me. The word triggered Gemma too. Her head snapped up from where she crouched over the body bag at the other side of the room. She straightened, glaring at me with daggered eyes until the coroner intercepted her and pulled her into the work.

Free to speak openly with Sett now, I beckoned him to follow me and pointed at the front door's brass knob. "Break-in. The lock looks like someone tried to pick it. Plus, according to what I've heard, Fate was a skilled electrical warlock. How did he scorch himself?"

Sett glanced around, his horns nearly scraping the top of the door frame. He stood with his legs wide, feet on either side of the threshold, one firmly inside and the other in the messy weeds next to me. "Interesting." Humming, he considered my theory while we scanned the entry and walked back to the study. Along the way, we stopped to look over Fate's belongings on the ground a few times. A thoughtful look crossed his face. "What I'm seeing is a place messy with raw wire. It doesn't look like he was being cautious."

"Based on the pattern of those wires, I know Fate was trying to recreate the spell," I said. "For protection. Maybe." Truly, I didn't know his motive for working on the spell. I didn't know the victim at all, in fact. But I knew that pattern, and I knew he was the last to look through *The Book of Prophecies* where the spell's pages were stolen.

Sett nodded. His gaze fell to the book and then flicked up to meet mine. The hard lines of his jaw softened. "Well, a break-in aligns with the abrasions on the victim's arms. It appears someone may have grabbed him. I wasn't going to jump to murder just yet since he could have gotten into a fight at another time. But I'll look into the possibility of a break-in."

He believes me. Warmth flooded my chest, and I nearly overheated. Thoughts of our almost-kiss at the fall festival came with the cozy heat. As Gemma approached, beads of sweat lined my brow, and I suddenly had the urge to run to the beach and dive in the frigid northern Californian water. Or I could lean into Sett to cool off at the touch of his chilly, statuesque skin...

I quickly buried the feelings. We'd almost kissed. *Almost.* Never made contact, never touched down, and I never regretted the absence of it, considering he'd arrested me. Sure, I'd broken the law, but it was for the sake of answers to uncover a killer. Since then, we'd remained friends. I forgave him for being so staunch, and he forgave me for my less-than-legal approach to solving last month's murder.

Still, the traitorous belly flutters cropped up here and there whenever he'd crack a smile. Or when he'd help Jovi practice soccer. Or when he'd vehemently argue—discuss—the funniest film of the year with me. *Liar Liar* or *Mousehunt*. Definitely *Mousehunt*, though I wasn't allowed to admit that in front of Squeaks.

"You're not needed here, Wolf." Gemma's pink lips settled in a hard line, and I almost mistook her harsh expression for a gargoyle's stony skin. But the human moved quicker than a gargoyle as she folded her arms across her chest and looked to the sheriff. "Lawrence? Won't you clear the crime scene?"

Sett's face twisted into an apologetic grimace. "Noema, thank you for answering the questions, but now I'll have to ask you to leave the investigation to law enforcement."

Fine. I have a spell to track down anyway.

I hugged the book to my chest and nodded. Before I spun around, I lowered my voice, an excuse to lean closer to the radiating chill from Sett's broad shoulders. Just a little closer and I could smell his leathery cologne... *No, curses!* How could my feelings betray me like that? This man had voted to cancel a whole family holiday for goodness' sakes.

And I was going to find a way to bring it back.

"I'll just check the rest of the house for the spell and then be on my way," I said, too quiet for Gemma to hear. Before Sett could object, the coroner ambushed both cops with new information, and I silently slipped out of the study.

My foot caught in a tangled Shadowvale University sweatshirt on the floor, but I swallowed a yelp and caught myself on the door frame. I glanced at the crime scene team and breathed a sigh of relief. They were still distracted, allowing me the freedom to snoop around the vacation home and sniff out the spell.

CHAPTER 5
IT'S A WARLOCK'S LIFE

SURPRISINGLY, it didn't take long to sweep the mansion. It was bare of items except for basic furniture, Fate's junk, and the books in the study that were all covered in dust and clearly untouched.

Since the missing pages weren't there, I resolved to go home, curl up with a bag of popcorn, and study *The Book of Prophecies*. Hopefully, I'd find clues on who'd created the grimoire. If they couldn't rewrite the spell, maybe they'd know why someone would want to steal it.

Over and over, the young witch's reaction popped up in my mind. She'd even mentioned Fate's attempt with the spell. It made the most sense that the only other witch in town had the pages. But why would she take it from Fate while he was working on it? And did that have anything to do with his death?

I shook my head. The murder investigation was for Sett and Gemma to solve, not for me to speculate about. I just wanted those missing pages and a fun holiday with a few pirates.

Once outside, I hugged the book closer and took another whiff of the peaceful scent. Despite the heavy clouds in the sky, the crackling tension of the murder investigation, and the hope-lessness of the lost pages, *The Book of Prophecies'* smell comforted me like a hug from a friend. Though I still didn't know where the scent came from without the protection spell's pages.

A gust of icy November wind swept unruly hair into my eyes. I shook it away before the momentary blindness had me colliding with a wire-framed pirate ship in front of the grocery. I skipped to the side in time to avoid crashing into the decora-tion. The rest of the shop was adorned with a dozen tiny pirate flags stuck into every flower pot that lined the ground outside the building. I hurried to retrieve the kids from Roller Shakes before the evening's chill got too cold, even for me.

Most of the roller rink patrons had gone home for the night, but the diner was still half-full of people grabbing a bite to eat or sharing a milkshake for dessert. Mae waved me over to the same booth we'd been sitting at only hours before. It felt days ago considering I'd stumbled upon a murder scene in the interim. I gave myself a little shake as if I were in wolf form and the memory of Fate's eyes was excess water I wanted to be rid of. The grandmotherly half-dragon greeted me with a million questions as soon as I slumped into the blue vinyl bench.

I told her about the missing pages and stopped there.

"I've watched enough *Dateline* and *Forensic Files* to know that worried look, honey. " She scooted closer to the table and perched her chin on her fists, eager for any juicy detail or gossip-laden bit of information. "You're not telling me some-thing, and you know as well as I do that I'm an asset to helping you find those pages." After a moment of silence, the only sound between us was the clink of the spoon. She stirred her tea and waited patiently.

I blew out a puff of air and relented, leaning comfortably onto the table to match her stance. "Here's what I know:

someone broke into the library through the window." It had to have been Fate since he was working on the spell, right? Then who killed him?

"Judy," Mae said as if answering my thoughts and pausing only to take a sip of tea, "must be throwing an absolute fit about the damage! She treats that library as if it was her very soul." She released a low whistle and stirred the tea again.

A prickling sensation spread over my scalp and my ears tucked back. Hadn't Judy threatened the library trespasser in front of me? She'd even punched the table just talking about it and then smelled of *guilt*. Air sucked from my lungs. Judy's emotions smelled awfully fishy when she claimed she'd only just arrived at the library. Had she seen the damage and left to confront Fate, pushing him into the wires for revenge? Why else would she lie about when she arrived at work?

With enough anger-fueled adrenaline, the slight librarian could have attacked the scrawny college kid, especially considering the little boost of natural physical strength passed down to her from her half-dragon ancestor. Of course, the odor of fish didn't only accompany lies. Sometimes guilt came from other sources. I had no real reason to suspect Judy of such a heinous crime, so I refused to jump to conclusions and be the impatient wolf I'd been in the past.

A figure in all black approached the table. Mae scooted to the side to let Crow sit, ever the welcoming grandmother of Bewitcher's Beach. When she wasn't gossiping, anyway. Crow nodded in gratitude and flashed her a side smile before raking his hand through his weighty curls.

Flutters danced in my chest when his dark eyes pinned me and his curved grin grew.

"We were just discussing the vandalism at the library," Mae filled him in, one eyebrow arched as she revealed the juicy tidbit. "Reminds me of what that college boy did to your

TVs here." Her attention shifted to me, red eyes wide. "Was it him?"

"Why do you say that?" I asked.

"Because he's a troublemaker, right Crow?" Mae asked. Crow tilted his head in a half-hearted nod. The thick waves of his hair fell to the side and shrouded one of his eyes. She continued without giving him a chance to chime in. "I remember Fate from when I sold that house to his family. His parents were quite prim. They'd be remiss to hear of his bad behavior. In fact, I'm surprised they ever let that boy stay at the vacation home without their supervision. He'd asked for his own key when they first purchased the home, but I overheard his parents refuse because he was too irresponsible."A twist of sadness curdled my stomach for the witch and warlock who'd soon be hearing of their son's demise. Mae sighed. "I'm willing to bet my retirement that he's the one who broke into the library. He probably had plenty of practice breaking into his family's house."

Family. The word reminded me of the kids I'd come here to retrieve as well as my goal with the protection spell. I twisted in the vinyl booth, my movements squeaking, and scanned the dwindling crowd in the rink. Mae and Crow's lively chatter muted to the background. My ears turned away and tuned in for the sound of Halen's bark or Stevie's squeals.

All four pups huddled around a skee ball machine. A clear Lisa Frank backpack full of Roller Shakes game tokens sat on the colorful carpet next to them. Halen and Dio chanted as Stevie stepped up to the rolling lane with her tongue plastered to the side of her mouth. Her gaze concentrated on the opening at the top where she could score one hundred points. Once she rolled the ball and it landed in the second highest scoring circle, they howled with cheers. The success earned them a few tickets that the machine spit out like a paper snake onto the floor.

The trail of paper tickets yanked my thoughts back to the grimoire's missing pages. Even if I did find them, Fate was no longer around to cast the spell. But what about the witch? Her worried voice popped into my head... *You tried the spell without me?*

I focused on Mae again. She polished off her tea with a satisfied sigh and then licked the glistening remains from her shimmering upper lip. "Do you know if Fate had a sister or a girlfriend, by any chance?" I leaned forward again.

The half-dragon hummed and shook her head. "Not that I remember."

"What about friends? Did you ever see him around town with a witch? Fashionable, friendly, about yea high." I held up my hand to show her approximate height.

"I—" Crow finally spoke up but Mae barreled over his words with an answer of her own. He relented and plucked a french fry off her forgotten plate, moving the dish in front of him as he listened.

"Did I *ever* see him." Mae's voice trailed, and she huffed a laugh. "Oh, honey. I don't let frequenters spend much time in this town before I get to know their inclinations. I have property to protect here. Of course I chatted with Fate and his friends from school a few times. I believe the fashionista witch you're referring to was one of his classmates. Sweet girl. Senna would come here to study with him. But I don't think she ever got involved in the drinking and partying like the rowdy ones did."

Swallowing, Crow interjected. He pushed the empty plate away and pointed at me with the fry in his hand. "That's probably the same witch he was arguing with here."

"Arguing?" My ears perked.

He nodded and chomped the fry, finishing it and wiping his hands clean with a napkin before explaining. He shifted forward, elbows on the table and hands clasped, speaking conspiratorially. "Late last night, I had to ask him and another young lady to quiet down. They were yelling about which one of them would keep a spell in their binder. The girl called it precious. To be honest, I thought they were drunk and I almost called Sett on them. I mean, *curses*, this is a roller rink."

Like me, Crow was a transplant to Bewitcher's Beach and clearly had not grown used to the idea that throwing around the "curse" word was unsettling to most Bewitched. It took all I had to bite my tongue before the curse slipped from my lips too. If they argued over the protection spell and it was missing from Fate's house, the mysterious young witch probably had it in her binder.

"Senna," I repeated with a nod and asked a few more questions. Neither Mae nor Crow knew the witch's last name or any helpful details about how to find her, but Mae insisted nobody knew more about Senna than she did. Except maybe Judy. As a librarian, Judy kept meticulous records of her patrons, and a college student surely frequented the quiet sanctuary of study and knowledge. "In fact," she said, red eyes gleaming, "I've seen the college kids using the computers there before. Judy practically requires a sacrifice and the name of their firstborn before a patron even breathes on the library's computers." The joke landed on deaf ears because Judy was scary enough for such a demand to be true.

A sigh escaped me as I nodded along. It made perfect sense, but Judy wasn't the person I wanted to go sniffing around for information from. I had unpleasant predictions of her grabbing me by the wolf's ears and twisting if I spoke too loudly in the library. "I suppose I'll have to get Senna's phone number from her."

"Oof." Crow's scar stretched as he mocked an exaggerated grimace. "Good luck with Judy. She's scary."

Mae hummed in agreement with his reaction. "Scary, yes, but she's your best bet for more information. What do you need from Senna, anyway?"

I stood and caught Jovi's eye, waving for him to tell his siblings and come meet me at the table. "I saw her in town tonight and I think she might be our only chance to cast the protection spell in time." My gaze fluttered to Crow for a moment, but I wouldn't let myself get distracted by his midnight eyes. "And based on that argument Crow heard, it sounds like she probably already has the spell."

It was a long shot—a long *hope*, really. But with a murderer prowling around town, I was sure the rest of Bewitcher's Beach would encourage the young witch to try the tricky spell and bring the protection back. If I was really lucky, she might have witnessed Fate working on it and already have an idea of how to get started. If only people with witches and warlocks in their bloodline could perform intention magic like the protection spell... Then we wouldn't have to wait for powerful witches to weave the complicated pattern.

Mae fanned Crow out of the way so she could scoot out of the booth, and we said our goodbyes. Before he stalked away, I grabbed his wrist. He froze, eyes fixed on my fingers around his arm until my cheeks heated and I yanked my hand back.

"You're warm."

It was all he said.

"Werewolf fever," I explained. "I'm always hot."

He casually dipped his hands into his pockets and a smirk danced on his lips as his gaze trailed over me. "I can see that. Why do you think I stopped working to come sit with you?" His voice dropped to a whisper and the smirk deepened. "Not for Mae's gossip, I'll tell you that."

Now my cheeks were fire, my forehead flames. My whole body burned, and I itched to wolf out and run from the compliment because I didn't know how to receive it. It'd been too long since anybody regarded me as attractive. I was merely a mom, a business owner, a friend.

Nobody had spoken to me like that since Christopher. Nobody noticed when I tied my curls back and let two strands frame my face. Nobody commented when I ventured to wear a dress or a little makeup. Not even Sett.

"I—uh." I cleared my throat and focused on why I'd grabbed him. "I just wanted to ask if you were out at the beach tonight. I thought I saw you."

His lips twisted down, considering this for a moment until he shrugged. "I was busy with work."

"Right." Of course he was. The roller rink was wild with business since the wind kept children cooped up inside.

AFTER GATHERING my pack of pups, we returned home to our little loft apartment above Mockbuster video rental.

Finally, I herded the distracted pups inside like a sheepdog and started the bedtime routine. They piled around me while I read Shel Silverstein's *Where the Sidewalk Ends* for approximately the seven-hundred and twentieth time.

Vanilla's scent of love surrounded us as we said goodnight, but Stevie's sad cries from before still plagued me. The six of us were family enough to celebrate. Seven, if I counted Sir Crabby.

Always enough.

But a cloud loomed in the back of my mind. What would

the holidays look like with grandparents and...did I have siblings? Did my kids miss out on meeting a 'cool' aunt or a pack of playful cousins? Did this unknown family miss me?

As I tucked each of my babies into bed, wrapped in the tattered strings of yarn from my terrible attempt at knitting, I pictured the Ghost Pirate Moon traditions. Hattie had described them to me since it only occurred once every decade and I wasn't in Bewitcher's Beach for the last celebration.

She'd said the entire town gathered on the shore where they welcomed the ship with dozens of bonfires. The fires represented the burning of past mistakes and forgiveness for any grudges among ancestors. It'd started because the pirates regretted their past lives of plundering and pillaging. They came ashore seeking forgiveness and praying to move on. When they found descendants who welcomed them without judgment here, the local residents decided to make the Pirate Moon a time of new beginnings where young brothers promised not to bicker over toys and grown sisters mended fences from long-ago rivalries.

And that was only the beginning of the familial celebrations.

On the last day, before the Drunken Oyster's tethered spirits were forced to return to sea, the entire town squeezed into the largest building—once The Oyster Inn with its name stolen from the pirate ship—and shared a feast of biscuits, beans, and salted beef. The spirits enjoyed the smells while the living had their fill.

I'd hoped to enjoy those smells too, but that was impossible unless I tracked down the stolen spell.

And track it down I would.

CHAPTER 6
THE SIXTH SCENTS

AS SOON AS snores drifted from the kids' bedroom, I slipped away, eager to dig clues from *The Book of Prophecies*. With a bottle of Diet Pepsi, a mixing bowl full of popcorn, and the book in front of me, I collapsed onto the sofa, where my rear end sank into the soft cushion.

It didn't take long before I scooted to the edge of the sofa and huddled over the open book. I scanned carefully, searching for anything that would help me track down the original author. If I could find the witch who wrote the spells, I wouldn't need to follow the stolen pages. I wouldn't need to risk irritating Gemma with putting my nose where it didn't belong or deal with Judy to get Senna's information.

There had to be a clue, something among the healing spells and soup recipes to tell me who'd created this book. Or what young warlocks and witches like Fate and Senna wanted from it.

I flipped to a prophecy. I'd never paid much attention to anything beyond the protection spell, but now was the time to dig, so I read slowly.

Hearts combined as one. Every witch under the sun who is of the drink of the gods divine. They are chosen as wives for the guides of lives to the beyond.

"Remind me to research what gods drink in the mythology books next time we go to the library," I told Squeaks. He flicked his tail in acknowledgment but didn't peep an eye open.

The blank space between "every" and "witch" caught my eye, as though words were erased, redacted, removed from history. I squinted, but no trace of letters were visible. Who were the guides' wives? I tabbed through the pages and tried to spot the phrase, stopping when I found the words above a sketch. The image portrayed a man who used a scythe as a walking stick. My gaze fell to the words beneath.

Guides of lives to the beyond: reapers are called to the dying. They walk them into the afterlife lest their spirits remain trapped and listless. Each reaper, man or woman, carries a scythe of various sizes to hook the spirit when it leaves the body and before they float away, lost to wander. Once reaped, the spirit will find rest, and the reaper will be shrouded as they return to their daily life between The Calling.

Though this wasn't getting me answers, I wanted to soak in every word of information in *The Book of Prophecies*. But the pull in my heart was more than curiosity. Something about the word "reaper" felt like home. It felt familiar. I returned to the text to see what else it might spark.

A reaper may be called to one close to death to prepare, but they cannot intervene and save a life or else the spirit will become entangled with the body. Once an intervened spirit does become lifeless whether immediately or in the future, it will be trapped in burial with the physical form, forever doomed. Reapers are humans chosen by The Unnamed Witch to serve exactly seventeen years reaping souls and not a day more. Once The Calling selects someone, they're bound to these rules.

I recalled the little scythe charm on the necklace of the reaper who ran Bewitcher's Beach's workout studio. The woman was a tyrant in her workout regime, always warning residents that their time on earth was short and they must move their bodies in order to extend their lifespans. As far as I knew, she was a retired reaper, and the scythe around her neck was nothing more than a memory of her past calling.

"You learn something new everyday. Isn't that right, Squeaks?" The mouse stirred and released a little grunt before settling back down. Whatever he'd said, I didn't know since Stevie wasn't awake to translate. Later, when I had more time, I'd study the section of the grimoire titled "Magical Animals and Their Abilities" to see if Squeaks qualified. He didn't have any powers to speak of, but behaved more like a person than any pet I'd ever met.

I pulled the book into my lap and leaned deeper into the comfortable, worn couch, and it flipped open to a page I hadn't seen before, past where the protection spell had once been. I'd never read this far. Never seen this prophecy scrawled in cursive ink. The first line drew me in immediately, and my breath hitched.

Ancestors of chosen witches will be marked, revealing the descendant. Each chosen one offers protection with magic of intent.

Marked like Senna was with the wing-like tattoo? I didn't

pause too long, again sucked into the words as if pulled by an invisible string.

One pirate, Annette, with skills of swords against every threat.

As soon as I reached the end of the sentence, a rush of smells assaulted me. Fish, mildew, the briny sea, and the spice of rum swirled around me. When I took a slight whiff, breathing deeper, my eyes still scanning the first sentence of the prophecy, a dizzy wave surged through my head and my eyes blurred. A daydream, no—a vision—popped into my mind to accompany the scents. A brunette pirate stood at the helm of a ship as wind whipped her hair. The ship docked, and she hopped out into the water, sloshing through the waves toward an approaching man to whom she offered her hand. He greeted her, addressing her as Annette, Captain of the Drunken Oyster.

I blinked the daydream away and blew out a breath. "My imagination is working overtime, Squeaks!" The wild visualization left my heart hammering. "Guess I'm too excited about getting the Ghost Pirate Moon party back..." I muttered as if speaking aloud would whisk the strange daydreams away. After a bite of popcorn, my head cleared, and I kept reading.

One mother Midnight, with the protection of foresight.

Another array of aromas surged as if from the pages, and another daydream swallowed me. For no longer than a moment, jasmine fragrance filled my nose, and I was lost in my mind, picturing a beautiful woman in an Edwardian forest green dress with a black corset surrounding her midsection. In a grove of trees, she sat with *The Book of Prophecies* in her hand. It was quite the image, and I shook it away quickly. Maybe it'd been too long since I'd sat down with a notebook and pencil and scribbled out my screenplay ideas. My brain was going rogue.

Finally, I tore my gaze away from the prophecy and fixed it on the television until the sudden smell faded and my overactive imagination calmed down. "I'm not crazy."

Squeaks chirped his disagreement as he curled back into a little ball and closed his eyes. This time I read aloud, whispering so as to not wake the grumpy mouse.

"One who weaves as a crafter, defenses for all that come after."

Another smell. Another daydream. "Oh no..." My breath was swept away as the smells and visions came simultaneously. This time, the scents were familiar—the same scent I thought I'd smelled from the protection spell. Smells of Christmas morning cinnamon bread, of rose perfume, and of wool yarn. This time, I was there as if reliving a moment from the past. A wrinkled hand wrapped a scarf around my neck, and I saw my own fingers lay the wool fabric flat over a 1980s neon pullover and stone-washed jeans. "My clothes..." I finally sucked air back into my lungs. "Those were my clothes." It was all I saw before the daydream, the vision—no, the *memory* came to an end.

Tears flooded my eyes as my hand, shaking, let go of the book and covered my mouth. Could it be? Was this prophecy somehow linked to me? Or was this a trick of the imagination once again? I shut the questions down and sped through the next few lines, suffering through the whiplash of memories and smells and emotions.

One who commands both winter and summer to split enemies asunder.

   One with the power of scent to smell a threat's intent.

"That's me!" I screamed. My hand slapped to my mouth again and my heart thump, thumped, the only sound in the room now besides the Pizza Hut commercial on TV. I dared to read the line again. Just like with the others, smells and memories flooded me. A memory from only nine years ago, when Christopher first told me he'd loved me. I'd smelled the vanilla around him, his emotion, his intent to love me forever. Shaking, I finished the prophecy, my finger barely able to follow along each line. The next sentence came with no smells, no memory.

One with the language of fauna and flora to lead defenses
against malevolent aura.
Each chosen for her skill, to shield innocents from those who kill.
Pirate.
Psychic.
Crafter.
Weathercaster.
Canine.
Communicator.
Each in a family with gifts to protect from every witch hater.
This is the prophecy of the Titan family.

"The Titan family. Is this *my* family?" I said it to the TV. To the silent room. To nobody.

I was alone while the kids snoozed softly in the next room and Squeaks slept. I'd never heard of the Titan family before, but I was sure to research the name now. If I couldn't find them, I had Annette. As the captain of The Drunken Oyster, she surely still haunted the ship. I could meet her spirit when the ghosts came ashore. I could meet an ancestor and ask her everything.

A buzz of energy rippled through me, and I couldn't keep my legs from bouncing. If I could shift into a wolf and swim out to the ship to meet her now, I would. Alas, I was in my fuzzy pajamas, and The Drunken Oyster was impossible to find until the new moon.

With every turn of the brittle pages, different smells mingled with the scent of my snack. I popped two pieces of popcorn into my mouth and tossed one to Squeaks. He perched on a pillow in front of the fireplace beside the TV. A new episode of *America's Funniest Home Videos* blared on the screen.

The host—a famous actor who starred in *Full House*, a show about families—only pricked my heart every time he mentioned family. His warm smile sparked a wave of grief for the man I'd lost and the family I couldn't remember.

Nobody else recognized me or could place me with a family anywhere near Bewitcher's Beach. Even Mae, the over one-hundred-year-old half-dragon, didn't relocate here until rumors of a paranormal protection spell spread far enough to call her and her husband to the shore. I'd been a werewolf, having forgotten my past self due to the transformation, since I turned sixteen nearly twenty years ago.

Grief quickly melted away with the spark of hope. I fluttered through the pages again, wondering what other phrases might catch my attention or smells surfaced.

I paused on a page that covered the magic business of summoning another being.

Roses, yarn, a snowflake, cinnamon pastries.

The list was curiously close to the memory I had of myself

in 1980s fashion and the old woman's hand. The vision was too unclear to see her face, but maybe this spell would tell me more about her.

> *Each personal object is to be set in a circle. These are a few of her favorite things and thus used to bring her forth by another's will but not requiring her own. One moment here, the next gone.*

My eyes flicked to the sketches and notes in the margins regarding summoning shapes. Summoning circles were to bring forth another and diamonds were meant to trap the target in case of threat.

I turned to the front of the book. Leaving the summoning spells behind, I blew out a breath. It didn't inspire any visions or memories, but it was surely connected.

Another sketched image caught my eye. I ran my hand over the drawing, brushing my fingertips against the brittle page with as much softness as a werewolf could muster. Two gently curved lines mirrored one another each with several jagged columns and four with taller, pointed peaks. I flipped to the page before to read the notes where other sketches —one of a reaper's scythe and another of bat-like wings— were drawn.

> *A mark will appear on the chosen one of her lineage. Once identified, the mark can be used to spell out the future, a prophecy for the future of a witch's family.*

What did the images mean? Unfortunately, as curious as I was, it gave me no answers about who'd created the book, who Senna might be, or why Fate had attempted the protection spell on his own, and with wires.

"Well the book's a bust for clues on the author," I said, trying to suppress my excitement about the memories.

I had to focus. I'd never heard anyone utter the name "Titan" before, but Annette was captain of a ship that was due to visit very soon—*if* I could find and reinstate the protection spell, which still required the help of a witch. Squeaks lifted his head and blinked sleepily at me. "We have to find Senna."

He squinted and then lifted his chin in a single nod before returning to his snuggled cinnamon roll position.

"I guess I'm stuck asking Judy for help." I'd hoped to avoid the same conclusion I'd come to at the roller rink. I snorted at the thought of Judy helping me with anything. She had held a grudge ever since Mockbuster's videos grew in popularity. Or so it felt based on her snide comments and death glares when we occasionally came in contact. I had no desire to cross paths with her unless absolutely necessary. Of course, the promise of the holiday celebration I'd made to my kids was necessary. Finding my family felt necessary too, and protecting Bewitcher's Beach? Definitely necessary. "Wait, maybe I don't need Judy to find Senna."

I sat up, and the popcorn bowl fell over the cushion's edge, leaving a salty mess across the shag rug. I had my own rentals with records! If the witch had ever borrowed a VHS tape from the shop, I'd have her info stored in the computer.

When I jumped up and swung open the door that led to the staircase, Squeaks released the sound of his namesake. I hurried down the spiral stairs that led directly into the shop where rows of VHS tapes lined the gray carpet. *New Releases* was splashed across the left wall that shared a door right into Everland Theater's backstage. To my right, racks of snacks, candy, popcorn bags, and more lined the wall and at the far end by the large front windows was the computer register and desk. I scooted behind it and booted up the system.

An hourglass symbol spun around on the computer's screen. After a moment, the register prompted me to scan a rental. Instead, I clicked out of the main page to the list of renters with Mockbuster cards, which was both a requirement to borrow a VHS tape and my insurance to track any lost rentals. Hopefully, it'd track lost witches too.

If Senna had dropped in on a busy day, I might have rung her up without so much as glancing up. I held my breath as the system searched for her name. The hourglass spun, spun, spun, and I tap, tap, tapped my foot until the computer loaded and said "no matches for *Senna*."

"Doggone it." I released the curse with a sigh and dropped onto the stool behind the desk. I had no choice but to risk the wrath of the *Livid Librarian*. I resorted to the nickname my pups had unaffectionately called Judy after we'd witnessed her yelling at a high school student for highlighting a library book. A shiver trickled through me.

I resolved to brave the library tomorrow and get Senna's information. The sooner we had the protection spell and a witch to cast it, the sooner we'd be safe from the murderer. If Sett and Gemma didn't uncover the spell in their investigation, it was most logical that the only other powerful wielder of magic—and Fate's classmate—had the spell.

Then, armed with the spell and with Senna's agreement, I'd crash tomorrow's meeting and convince the town to vote that the holiday celebration commence under the safety of the returned protection.

First, I had to get past Judy and live to tell the tale.

CHAPTER 7
THE BEWITCHED CLUB

EARLY THE NEXT MORNING, before opening Mockbuster, I dragged four tired kids in their pjs and raincoats to the library. We tried to speak with Judy only for her to kick us out over our wet dog smell. And when I tried to request Senna's information, Judy insisted she had nothing of the sort.

My back up plan didn't work either. None of the customers I slipped Senna's name to had any clue who she was, where she'd come from, or where she stayed during her time in Bewitcher's Beach. Despite the setback, I kept asking and kept digging, keeping my eye on the protection spell prize.

The torrential rain could not stop Mockbuster's business from booming. The storm didn't deter fairies and half-dragons, gargoyles and shapeshifters, humans and reapers from braving the swirling wind and sheets of rain for a few hours of entertainment on their TV. They came in droves, renting stacks of VHS tapes for a Friday family night, a dinner and a movie date, or to pass the time while stuck indoors. Even vampires, protected from the sun by the thick cloud cover, rose from their coffins to face the day and rent a film before I closed up shop.

I'd posted a piece of paper on the glass last night, warning that Mockbuster wouldn't be available during the town meeting tonight.

Mockbuster's phone rang off the hook until I finally had a moment to answer.

Mae greeted me from the other line as I twisted the phone's spiral cord around my fingers. "In the interest of supporting your protection spell idea, I've reached out to Judy and kindly requested Senna's information. She only agreed to share her phone number."

"What?" Both excited about the news and disturbed by Judy's lie, my pulse skittered off beat. Thanks to the rain washing away smells, I hadn't even caught a whiff of fish or ammonia from Judy's guilt or nerves. "She told me she didn't have Senna's phone number."

Mae hummed. "Well that certainly can't be the case because I'm looking at the number right now and, in fact, I called it myself this very morning and left her a message. Just to test it, you know? I always see the agents and detectives in my shows double-check their leads." A man's voice interrupted Mae, and she mumbled something to her husband about bringing her famous meat pie to the meeting before she returned to the phone and relayed the phone number. "I'll see you tonight. Good luck, honey. You know I'll be voting for the holiday to continue. I can't bear the thought of disappointing all the youngins in town who have yet to experience the joys of the Ghost Pirate Moon. Not to mention the salted beef. It tastes like—"

"Duck!" Jovi screamed as a soccer ball whizzed past my head and slammed into the wall behind the register. It bounced off the wall, jarring the display of candy nearby, and then hit the register, knocking Squeaks from his beauty sleep where he was curled on the top of the warm computer.

I bid Mae goodbye, replaced the phone on the receiver attached to the wall, and clucked my tongue. "That's enough indoor soccer. You'll end up breaking a window or hitting a customer."

I sent the kids upstairs while I phoned Senna. The other line rang and rang and rang until a robotic voice offered for me to leave a voice message. I explained the situation, carefully highlighting the need for the protection spell.

After I tried several more times and Senna never answered, it was left to a hope and a prayer that she'd show up to the meeting with the spell in hand.

As evening approached, the glow of the lamp posts that lined Bewitcher's Beach's cobblestone streets blinked on. I stood at Mockbuster's glass door and watched as the rain still pelted the ground, soaking the grass in the center park and creating puddles in the grooves of the uneven sidewalk. Thanks to the meeting, customers dwindled the closer the clock crawled to the scheduled time. Everyone hurried home to drop off their loot of VHS tapes and eat a bite before arriving at The Oyster Inn to vote for the holiday.

At least I hoped the majority would vote for the holiday once they heard my plan for safety and protection from possible poltergeists.

A shimmering ghost appeared in the dark of the rental shop and floated through the rows of movies.

"Hi Hattie." I greeted my best friend and next door neighbor, the 1920s Hollywood starlet who haunted Everland Theater with her teenage daughter Bette. Actually, she haunted the emerald from a piece of old costume jewelry, but she spent most of her time among the tattered red chairs and the worn wooden stage. She longed to return to Hollywood, and I longed to go with her—as a screenwriter, not an actress. Between her connections and one day hopefully turning the theater into a movie screen and garnering enough of an audience for my amateur films, we'd convince an agent to come to a screening. But those dreams were years away. For now, we were simply partners at the theater who bickered like sisters.

Hattie rolled her eyes as she phased through the front door that was still closed. I opened it and followed her on our way to the town forum. "Don't 'hi Hattie' me when I know you asked Bette to babysit again. If you keep giving her money, she's going to waste it on art supplies. She just wants to get that vampire boy's attention who's always sketching in the park at night." She waved her hand across the street at a dimly lit bench in the park. Rain passed right through her thinly manifested body.

"Bette likes art."

She huffed and curled her lip. The expression looked elegant on her angular face. Her blonde bob swished at her chin, and she pursed her ruby lips. The shimmer of her glittering flapper girl dress occasionally caught the light and sent golden reflections dancing on the ground beneath her. "Bette likes boys. And their attention."

"Didn't you at that age?" I hugged *The Book of Prophecies* closer to my chest where it was safely tucked under my purple wind-breaker. Hurrying away from the rain, we darted across the narrow alleyway and under the overhang at The Oyster Inn.

The ghost mimicked the sound of blowing out breath though she had no lungs. "Of course I did. Where do you think Bette came from?" She flashed me a wry smile. "Speaking of men, and since you claim that you and Sett are only friends, is your *deal* with Crow any deeper than a movie trade?"

Heat rose to my cheeks. "Why would you ask that?"

"Because he's looking at you like you've made the storm stop and called forth the sun with your bare hands." She lifted her chin at the approaching figure with a tilted grin. Crow's dark eyes fixed on me as he jogged to The Oyster Inn's front door. Opening it, he beckoned for us to pass through first.

Hattie winked at me before she phased right through the wall and left us alone at the threshold. With Crow close behind, I stepped into the inn and pulled the book out from under my jacket.

"Noema Wolf, fancy meeting you here." His grin wavered when his gaze dropped to *The Book of Prophecies*. The scar that hooked his cheek curved like a half-moon when he finally smiled again. "That grimoire is fascinating, isn't it? I've looked at it for recipes in case Roller Shakes could use a menu upgrade. Anyway, did you find the spell you wanted?"

"Not yet," I said as I scanned the lobby for any sign of a fashionably dressed witch.

Warm light glimmered from the twinkling chandelier. Barney had procured it from the fairy realm to brighten The Oyster Inn's lobby on even the darkest of evenings. Crystals caught the yellow glow and cast elegant sparkles around the room, bouncing off of the pristine wood floor.

There was no sign of Senna, but I spotted a gargoyle, a fairy, and the mayor, who sat at the bar to the right of the lobby.

"Sett Lawrence," I shouted and marched across the slick, freshly-mopped floor, Crow at my heels.

A pixie no larger than my arm flitted behind the tall counter and poured Pepsi into a frosted glass. Sett wrapped his stony fingers around the handle and slowly twisted his neck to meet my gaze. I wrinkled my nose at the slice of lime on his glass. As good as it smelled, I *hated* the taste of lime and nearly gagged at the sight of it on his drink.

Of course he liked lime. Of course he ruined an already-perfect drink with that rubbish. Of course... because he and I were exact opposites. His gargoyle skin was about as cold as the frost on his icy mug while my werewolf body burned at a heightened temperature. He followed every meticulous rule, and I skirted outside the law in the name of justice. When he took his time, I ran. And despite every difference, my heart still skipped a beat as his slate eyes found mine. The harsh gray skin wrinkled with a faint smile—a smile only I could recognize beneath his severe gaze. "Noema, how can I help?"

My eyes dropped to the bubbling soda in his hand, and a sneeze overcame me.

"Maybe consider hearing Noema out before you ask the town to vote," Crow answered before I could speak. The bite in his voice almost convinced me he was a vampire. A belief backed by his bloodlessly pale skin and sharp features. But the rhythmic thud of his heartbeat pricked my keen hearing and proved that theory wrong.

"I'd be happy to listen. I always appreciate Noema's ideas." Sett met Crow's smug smirk with a deadpan glance.

That was a *lie.* I resisted the urge to roll my eyes. Sett disagreed with me more than a few times. Despite the erratic thudding in my chest, I explained my plan. I already knew what he'd say based on the crack of concern between his eyebrows. I already knew Sett chose rules and security over the risk of love or kindness or friendship. I already knew because he'd arrested me when I'd only broken the law to solve the case he'd fallen behind on. To him, policy and procedure ruled, even snuffing out the person who cared for him.

Doggone it. I don't care what Sett Lawrence does as long it's not canceling the invitation.

When I finished, he responded with a sigh. "It's a solid plan if you can get the spell and have it cast again. But that's a big 'if.' The ghost pirates are always a risk since some lose themselves to poltergeist activity. Now that we're all exposed, it's even more dangerous." His voice trailed away.

"Enough is enough," Barney said. The elderly fairy's wrinkles folded in on themselves, and his jowls fell in a deeper frown. He yanked his brown cardigan tighter across his chest and huffed. "I don't want those dumb ghosts scaring away tourists. I've had it up to here"—he cupped his jaw where patchy gray fuzz covered his chin and then shoved his full glass of sparkling water away from him—"with the protection spell and festivals and ghost reunions. Nothing draws a visitor like a good old fashioned walk on the beach or a quiet town to sit and have a spot of tea. These extras are just fodder for drama."

Mayor Fitz chimed in, his grin never wavering in the face of Barney's moaning and groaning. "While that's true, festivals and reunions are for the happiness of Bewitched citizens." He stood after he said his piece, stretching to his full height of five feet with the help of heeled boots. Light reflected off his shiny head to match the beam of his smile as he waved at someone behind me.

Sett's gaze followed and he nodded a slight greeting.

I glanced over my shoulder after the welcome bell chimed again and a stream of familiar faces filed in. Soon, dozens of Bewitcher's Beach residents filled the quaint lobby to a tight squeeze. Gemma arrived behind Mae and Wallace, ducking away from the half-dragons with an annoyed look on her face. Likely they were trying to talk her ear off, and she only had eyes for Sett as she crossed the lobby and confidently took a seat at the bar beside the sheriff.

"Glad you could make it to the forum, Gemma," the mayor said, still smiling. "We missed you at the prep-meeting yesterday afternoon."

"I had paperwork to finish at the station," she said as she

swung one leg over the other, sitting cross-legged and following suit with folded arms.

When the mayor turned to me, he gently cupped my arm. "Anyway, I think what Barney is trying to say is that he'll be voting against the invitation. But you're free to counter his argument with a vote of your own." Fitz dipped his head and then ducked between me and Crow. "Will you excuse me? I heard someone call my name." He followed the crowd as townspeople shuffled into the dining hall past the bar. The bartending pixie had swung the double doors wide open, inviting vampires and sirens and ghosts inside. Accompanying Mae and Wallace was another friend who worked as a roller-skating server at Crow's diner, Cordelia. The vampire crossed the threshold into the dining hall with her husband and son in tow.

I followed the crowd into the room of a dozen round tables and a small stage where the pixie plucked strings on a minia-ture harp. With Barney in charge, this town forum was sure to be classy and offer a glimpse into what life was like in the fairy realm—all about music and beauty to counter the ugliness of cold hard truth.

I scanned the sea of faces, but Senna was nowhere to be found.

As soon as I found a seat, Mayor Fitz hopped onto the stage and got down to business. Announcements went quickly, paving the way for the debate to begin. Barney and Sett said their piece, and Cordelia stood, her toddler son on her shoul-ders, and countered their statements.

"But," Sett started, slate eyes on the vampires, "as an undead family, you're at less of a risk than many of your neigh-bors. The protection spell stopped you from being destroyed by rogue supernatural hunters, but you're not in danger from a poltergeist like the rest of us."

Without taking my daggered gaze off the sheriff, I folded my arms and whispered a rebuttal. "Wrong. A poltergeist can send a stake flying through a vampire's heart as easily as a hunter." *Wait.* That only proved his point. I growled and glanced at the wide open doors, hoping Senna would sweep in at any second with the spell in hand.

But the witch wasn't in the doorway, and all I had to show for my plan was a book with a stolen spell.

Ammonia mingled in the air—the scent of fear emanating from a few townspeople. Townspeople who were nodding along and agreeing with Sett's plan for the Ghost Pirate Moon invitation. Another smell joined the ammonia, almost overpowering the stinging scent— a smell that only further steeled my resolve to counter the votes. The earthy aroma of rain filled the room, matching the sadness on everyone's frowning faces.

"It's decided then." Mayor Fitz's grin wavered for a moment. He swiped his palm over his shining bare head and clapped his hands. "Time to take this to a vote. We will continue the holiday as tradition demands, or the invitation will be canceled for this November's new moon and we will not help the ghost pirates find their way ashore."

"Not if I have anything to do with it," I muttered. With all the energy in the world, I lifted the anchor weighing in my chest and mustered a smile. I stood and raised my voice to a bark. "We don't have to do that."

Heads twisted, people spun around in their chairs, the pixie stopped plucking the instrument's strings. All at once, I thought I'd wet my pants. The smell of ammonia rose pungent and burning in my nose, my own fear suddenly triggered by a moment I'd never forget. Only a few weeks earlier, these same faces stared at me, blinking and afraid that I'd cast a curse on the VHS tapes at my rental shop and murdered a customer.

I forced a swallow, but my swollen throat and heavy tongue

nearly choked me. My fingernails prickled as they stretched and grew into claws. The fur on my ears spread, growing over my flesh. Any second, I'd have to drop to all four paws before I lost my balance. Adrenaline flooded me, and my body reacted without my permission.

I bit my tongue. *Not now. These people aren't a threat!* Still, I felt foolish demanding their attention and trust when I had neither the spell nor the witch to cast it.

"Noema?" Sett prodded. Concern creased his broad forehead.

Tick. Tick. Tick. I filled my cheeks with air and pushed my breath out through circled lips.

"The spell," I finally said.

"Is missing!" Judy screeched angrily from the other side of the room. The red-headed librarian shot to her feet like a rising flame.

"That's true, but it can't have left town. Nobody has been able to get in or out. I believe I know who might have it."

The pixie spoke up from her perch on the harp. "What does that matter? Only a true witch has the power to cast intention magic, and no true witches live in Bewitcher's Beach."

"You're certainly right." Barney nodded to his musician. "We're supposed to be waiting for Madam Rowena, someone with enough skill and practice to come cast it so that no mistakes are made! I'm not willing to risk anything getting messed up around here." He met my gaze with a grimace. "Again."

"Actually." I returned his gaze with narrowed eyes and responded in a firmer voice. "There's a student in town from Shadowvale University. I spoke with Senna last night, and I believe she might have the spell. Or at least might have watched someone else try to recreate it." I quickly scanned the crowd for any sign of recognition at the mention of her name.

Nobody looked particularly alerted by it. I sniffed for a whiff of anything telling, but the scents in the room were the same: stagnant. Emotions were paused as they waited for me to finish the explanation. "Just give me time to contact her before we make any rash decisions. We have nine days until the Drunken Oyster appears on the horizon and the spirits need the guidance of the lighthouse to invite them to shore. Allow me just a few of those days to get this figured out and for Senna to study the spell."

Sett shook his head and leaped to his feet, a rare sighting of him moving faster than molasses. "I'd prefer to wait for the professional."

"Me too!" Barney shouted as he slapped his knee.

The chair next to me groaned as it slid across the floor. Crow backed away from the table and stood as a silent, tall, and dark force beside me. "Personally, I'm with Noema and not even because of the holiday. There is danger here in Bewitcher's Beach."

Gemma rolled her eyes before leaning over and whispering something to Sett. How dare she roll her eyes at the mention of danger? The odor of jealousy swirled around me as an unpleasant reminder of my bias. I wanted to suspect her of something nefarious, wanted her to have a motive. But she didn't.

I flicked my gaze over Crow and noticed his hand was nervously fiddling with something in his coat pocket. Had word of Fate's murder already gotten back to Roller Shakes and spooked Crow?

"Yeah!" A small voice echoed from the front of the room. Heads twisted and eyes squinted to see the child standing at the front. Apparently Noodle's parents had brought him to the meeting because the little shapeshifting kid stuck in the form of an octopus was proudly facing the whole town. He balanced on seven tentacles while the eighth held a slice of a sushi roll—which felt wrong considering his sea-creature shape. His dad jogged to the front of the room and tried to quietly guide Noodle back to his seat, but the kid was having none of it. "I saw the police at our neighbor's house last night, and they carried out a body bag!"

Gasps rippled through the townspeople, and the room erupted into a buzz of energy and conversation.

Mayor Fitz nodded. "Well I didn't want to frighten everyone with news of a heinous crime before it was more fully investigated, but I can see it is too late for that. Let's get the protection spell reinstated by any means possible and get my people comfortable!"

Sett stood and raised his hands, trying to quiet the crowd before he slowly twisted his neck to meet the mayor's gaze. "We're working on the investigation, and it appears to be targeted. We have no reason to believe anybody else is in danger."

"With all due respect, Sheriff," Mayor Fitz said, an unwavering grin on his ever-positive face. "If the people feel safer with the protection spell, then let's get that protection spell sooner rather than later."

"That's all fine and good," he said, voice harsh and determined, "but it's my job to protect the people you speak of, and there's no guarantee the spell will be up and running before the new moon. We're here to weigh the risks of the Ghost Pirate holiday and vote—"

"Then let's see what the vote decides," I said, eyes now fixed on the sheriff who utterly irritated the fur off of me. More than once, he'd gotten in my way. My cheeks burned from a memory of the last time he was in my way. I'd run into him and accidentally shifted from my wolf form to my human body, leaving me momentarily naked at his feet. I shook off the image and focused on Mayor Fitz as he stood and called for the official vote.

"All in favor of Noema's plan—"

Before the mayor could finish, nearly every single hand shot into the air. My heart danced a giddy jig in my chest until I remembered I still had to find Senna...and the spell.

CHAPTER 8
WHEN CROW MET NOEMA

WHILE THE PUPS watched an array of Saturday morning cartoons from *Doug* to *Pinky and the Brain* with Hattie's teenage daughter, we moms enjoyed a breakfast of bacon, Diet Pepsi, and coffee. Well, the coffee was for Hattie. Once she had her fill of the nutty and chocolatey scent, I poured the drink down the drain because I preferred the syrup and bubbles of soda to the buzzing anxiety that came with the doubled amount of caffeine from coffee.

Like the two mice on the kids' television show, Hattie and I discussed a plan to track down Senna.

"If she doesn't call you back, how will you find her?"

"She frequents the library," I said as I stood over the stove and opened a second package of bacon. The pan sizzled with each new strip I laid down, and Hattie floated closer, taking a whiff of the meaty aroma. I faced her and leaned my hip against the counter. "I'm going to hang out there for the day to see if she shows. I asked Judy about it after the meeting last night, and she said Senna comes by when it's slower on Saturday afternoon and late on Sundays."

The edge of her high cheekbones sharpened with the purse

of her lips. "Are you doing this for the kids or because you hope you're related to someone on that ship?"

The pups burst into a buzz of laughter at a joke in the cartoon. I stretched my neck just enough to see through the door and into the other room. "Honestly? Both. The kids don't want to miss out, and I keep getting memories every time I read the prophecy. If I could just meet Annette, maybe she'd recognize me. Or at least give me some family names to look into."

Hattie's brows disappeared beneath the curt line of her short bangs. "And because of the memories, you believe you're part of the prophecy?"

When she put it like that, it felt presumptuous. The scent of my embarrassment mingled with the bacon. I shook it off with a wiggle. "Not just the memories. I smell specific scents tied to some of the spells and recipes too. Plus, the prophecy mentions a canine with the ability to smell others' intentions. That has to be me." My stomach roiled with anticipation, groaning at the delicious grease bubbling in the pan. Hattie's silence spoke volumes, and my excitement was quickly dampened. "Just say it," I snapped. "Tell me I'm crazy and this is all in my imagination. I know you're thinking it."

To my surprise, she shook her head, and the swish of her silky blonde hair moved in time with the tiny golden tassels that covered her dress. "You're crazy, for sure. But not because of that. I'm merely concerned about how disappointed you'll be if Annette has become a poltergeist and refuses to talk to you. Poltergeists attack. They don't hang around and chat about family history."

My shoulders sagged with the weight of this truth. "You're not wrong, but do you always have to be so blunt about it? Is it so hard to say, 'Hey Noema, you're right and a genius and my best friend so I support you one hundred percent.'"

She tapped her red lips with a translucent finger. "Yes, it's terribly hard because I don't lie. And I've met more than a few poltergeists. They're all drama and death because they're angry that they've been trapped here for so long."

I rolled my eyes. "Drama and death? You and Barney would make a great couple, you know that?"

"Because he's a fairy and cannot lie?"

"Because you both see everything exciting as drama."

She gave me a deadpan stare, but I broke our gaze, choosing to focus on flipping the bacon instead of facing her. "Poltergeists are not exciting; they're violent and dangerous."

"And one particular poltergeist—or ghost—might be my only chance at finding my family," I said, hand on my hip with the spatula dripping grease onto the kitchen floor. I'd asked about the Titan family around town, even braving Judy, but had yielded nothing. Nobody recognized the name or knew more about the chosen witch prophecy.

With that, Hattie shook her head and phased through the wall where the landline phone was attached.

A knock rapped at Mockbuster's door downstairs.

Hattie's harsh voice had shifted to a singsong tune as she yelled to me on her way out. "There's a tall, dark, and handsome visitor here to see you, Noema." Thanks to the ghost's ability to walk through walls, she was able to phase through the floor and see who was at the door before I could so much as blink.

Had my cheeks warmed, or was I standing over the stove for too long? I knew exactly to whom she referred. Crow stood a foot taller than me, had curling dark hair that hung over his forehead, and was—as Hattie described—a regular Cary Grant. I begged to differ. Crow's hair was unrulier than the sleek polish of Cary Grant's style, and his facial scar gave him a perpetual smirk that was more mysterious than the actor's classy grin.

I wiped my greasy hands on a dish towel and tossed it on the scuffed table before hurrying downstairs. Crow's midnight eyes met mine through the glass door, and we exchanged smiles. The curve of the scar on his cheek looked like a scythe. Or perhaps a pirate hook.

You've got pirates on the brain, Noema.

I unlocked the latch and greeted him, hoping I didn't smell too much like greasy breakfast meat.

"I know it's not business hours, but I've never been great with normalcy," he said. "Is it too early to grab a movie?"

I opened the door wider and waved for him to step inside. "Let me guess, you watched the first *Back to the Future* at Roller Shakes and now you need the sequel?"

Crow's angular jawline tightened as he pursed his lips and narrowed his eyes at me. "I suppose you see through me as easily as I do you."

I shrugged and returned the smile that spread across his face again, though the comment was a little odd. "Maybe we're just alike. It was a guess based on what I'd do if I was at the roller rink all day with those TVs everywhere."

After we retrieved *Back to the Future* 2 from the science fiction section, he followed me to the register. His wiry muscles, though lean, bulged when he folded his arms across his chest, covering the logo of his black *Microsoft* T-shirt.

I tapped my foot again, waiting for the slow computer to switch back from the records to the register mode. "Sorry, this hunk of junk is slower than—" I stopped myself from saying Sett. Why did he even pop into my mind again, and right now? "Molasses."

Crow tilted his head and shuffled to the side to see the screen. "I could take a look at it sometime if you'd like." He pointed to his shirt with both thumbs. "I know a thing or two."

"Oh! Past job?" I asked. The computer finally caught up, and I scanned the rental and swiped his membership card.

"Yep." He nodded. I followed him to the door to lock it behind him. At the threshold, he froze and turned to face me, leaning with one arm against the frame. All of the focus in his dark eyes encompassed me. "Look, I also came by because I didn't get a chance to ask you this last night. I was hoping you and I could watch this together." He held up the VHS tape when movement on the sidewalk behind him caught my eye.

My gaze drifted to Gemma's swishing ponytail. Her hair was slicked back with half a tube of gel and pulled so tightly it looked as if the hairstyle gave her a face lift. The cop nodded her acknowledgment of us as she passed by, ticketing a delivery truck parked at the curb. Next, she moved to write up a fine for a pirate decoration that was an inch over the edge of the sidewalk.

I resisted the urge to stop her. These little details may have been breaking rules, but they were normal around here. Nobody cared that the delivery truck blocked the street because most of Bewitcher's Beach was devoid of cars and the residents walked everywhere. And the pirate decorations? They brought joy, not annoyance. Unless you asked Barney.

"I'm sorry." I shook my head, distracted. "Did you want to rent something else?"

He chuckled and swiped a lock of hair away from his eye before looking up to meet my gaze again. "No, I—uh, was wondering if you'd like to go on a date...with me?"

The question he dared ask swept my breath away. Peppermint scent surrounded me. To temper the nerves fluttering in my chest, I broke our gaze and found Gemma eyeing us with an arched eyebrow. She looked us up and down, and it was then I realized Crow was leaning on the door frame where I stood at the threshold. We were only inches apart. To the cop, it might look like we were about to perform a too-public display of affection. Not that openly kissing was illegal in Bewitcher's Beach, but *I'd* certainly never done it. In fact, I hadn't kissed anyone since Christopher.

"Noema?" Crow said, snapping me back to the here and now.

"I—" My jaw clamped shut. I'd sworn off love after my husband—my soulmate—passed. But this wasn't love, merely a date and a night of company while watching a great movie. I needed a little company, especially if Sett got his way and the holiday was canceled. It'd feel good to enjoy a bit of romance. Besides, if Sett and Gemma got back together after looking so chummy during last night's meeting, I'd lose my science fiction movie-watching buddy. I smiled up at Crow. "I'd love to."

Straightening, he stood a little taller, and a relaxed smile crossed his face. Now that it was official, the butterflies in my belly took flight, and I suppressed a goofy grin, acutely aware of the cop's prying eye.

After we discussed details of the date, Crow left and Gemma stopped giving me suspicious looks. My spirits lifted, and I shouted to Bette upstairs that I'd be back from the library soon.

If today's good luck continued, Senna would be at the library and she'd agree to give the protection spell a try.

CHAPTER 9
SMELLBOUND

THE LIBRARY'S musty sweet smell was dimmed by the heavier scent of fresh wood. I scanned the planks nailed into the wall where the boarded window now blocked the elements from further damaging the inside.

Judy didn't so much as greet me. When I requested the records, she sighed and crouched to pull out the giant box. In no hurry, she methodically ticked through the notecards until her finger paused at a card labeled P for *prophecies, the book of*.

Where the dangling parrot earrings had hung, she now wore tiny skulls and crossbones from her ears. The hollow eyes of the skulls stared into my soul as they swung against Judy's taut cheeks.

Senna had yet to drop by the library, so I busied myself by returning *The Book of Prophecies* and asking who else had requested it.

"I really don't see how this is any of your business," she muttered as she adjusted another pair of fake glasses, this pair with the frames in the shape of a cat's head. The pointed ears on each side poked into her partially-drawn eyebrows when she pressed the glasses against her face like they'd stick to her skin.

"I just want to find the missing pages," I said. "Before the new moon comes and goes and we miss our chance to meet the ghosts."

Judy peered at me from behind the counter with one eyebrow arched. "Have you ever even celebrated a Ghost Pirate Moon?"

"No," I admitted.

"So you don't know if you have any family members on the ship?"

"No." I winced.

She grunted and straightened with the notecard cupped in both hands, making no attempt to offer it over. I mustered a smile, and she finally thrust it out. "Don't take my copy. Make your own."

I skimmed the names. If the crime of the stolen spell and the attack were related, the person who'd taken the pages likely knew Fate had them in his possession. "One of these people could be a killer," I muttered. Of course, I wasn't here for that, just for the suspect with the spell. *Fate Kalabar, Senna James, Crow, Noema Wolf, Sett Lawrence, Gemma Stone, Judy Knovel, Noema Wolf, Noema Wolf, Noema Wolf.*

Apparently, I'd requested it more than anyone else. Even Crow only needed one look to gather recipes for Roller Shakes's menu. My memory wasn't great, but it was the comforting smell and curious images that kept me coming back over and over. What did Sett want with it? Did he hope to learn more ways to protect Bewitcher's Beach? Or maybe he wanted to bring it back and with the help of his partner against crime. With Gemma's name next to his, I wouldn't be surprised if they discussed using the spell as an asset for citizen safety. Knowing Sett, he'd taken it as his lawful duty to reinstate the woven, magical protection.

"Something wrong?" Judy's judgmental tone sliced through

my thoughts, cleaving the theory in half. I glanced up to see her searing gaze across the desk. "You're baring your teeth, Ms. Wolf. I'd ask you kindly to keep your aggressions under wraps in this sacred place of knowledge."

Was I really baring my teeth? I licked my lips and quickly quieted the growl growing in my chest. Did it bother me that much to see Gemma and Sett's names side-by-side?

I shook it off, turned the card over, and continued scanning. *Judy Knovel, Noema Wolf, Noema Wolf, Noema W—*.

I thrust the card back toward her. I'd seen enough. My mind reeled. Judy had even recorded her own request for the book. I had to give it to her, she was nothing if not meticulous, but couldn't she just look at it while she was here working?

That left one likely spell-stealing suspect—Senna—and now I had a last name with which to find her.

"Ms. Wolf!" Judy roared. The smoky smell of anger flared, even stronger than her usual cloud of irritation whenever I came near. "I don't appreciate being stared at like a TV screen! My goodness." She huffed and pulled her long sweater tighter across her chest, hugging it closely. "A blank stare like that can only have one source of blame—a mind melted by screens."

I blinked and stiffened. Her hatred for movies and Mockbuster only seemed to grow by the second. Or was she mad because I wanted to find the pages and she was the one who kept them hidden? But for what purpose? As far as I knew, Judy had a one-track mind: books, books, and books about books, which didn't link to tampering with a protection spell and the warlock trying to recreate it. Unless she went into a rage when she discovered Fate had torn a sacred book. If she'd hidden the pages, it was because they'd trace back to her anger-induced crime.

The scowl souring her face only further proved the theory in my mind. Still, Senna was suspect number one for the spell.

If Judy murdered Fate over a damaged book, Gemma and Sett would be the ones to find out, not me.

"Sorry," I mumbled, not wanting to get on her bad side. Becoming her next victim was not on my to-do list. I offered her the notecard and pointed to the shelf above her head. "You can add my name again, I'd like to request another look."

"Again?" Judy's top lip pinched and peaked in disgust, but she retrieved *The Book of Prophecies*, carefully climbing down from the ladder with it cupped under one arm.

After securing the grimoire in my hands, I plucked a book about bats from the nature aisle. I retreated to a table in the back of the library as far away from her watchful eye as possible. The cozy library didn't offer enough space to put a comfortable distance between us, but at least she couldn't glare at me behind a short wall that offered a quiet and individualized study space.

Judy muttered to herself, but I tried to block out the snide remarks. "Maybe if she didn't watch so many movies, she could manage a book without pictures."

Ouch. One of these days, I'd show Judy a great book-to-film adaptation and prove to her that both mediums can coexist peacefully. But today was not that day, and she had a point about the picture books.

I shrugged and flipped open to the sketches—or the *pictures,* if Judy had any say in it. Scanning the marks that appear on chosen witches, I then cross-referenced the images with a photograph of a vampire bat in the nature book.

The door slammed, nearly jolting me out of the seat. I peered over the privacy wall and swallowed a gasp in my throat. Senna marched into the library, stomping across the carpet with the chunky heels of her purple oxford shoes that matched the shade of her plaid mini skirt and blazer. The witch looked as though she'd just stepped out of a TV screen playing *Clueless.*

"Hey—"

"Shh!" Judy shushed Senna.

Senna cleared her throat and started again at a much lower volume. "Any chance you know if the human who runs the roller rink has a warlock in his bloodline?"

The ground wavered beneath me as the unexpected question left me dizzy. Why was Senna asking about Crow?

Judy huffed. "I am a guide of information regarding bound texts. Not a gossip station. If you'd like a book about roller rinks or family heritage, I can point you to aisle—"

"Jude, please."

Jude? Were they friends? I carefully closed *The Book of Prophecies* and scooted the chair back.

"I-I was just hoping to talk with him, and he wasn't at work." She released a loud sigh, and Judy shushed her again.

"To answer your question, no, I've no idea if Crow is part warlock. But if you think he had any part in ripping the book, you must send him here to be punished properly. Got it?"

Punished? A shiver stole down my spine. The possibility that Judy had pushed Fate into those wires was becoming more probable by the second. At least in my mind.

"Yeah, no, I'm not doing that," Senna said. "You seriously need to take a chill pill, Jude. I'm not here to punish anyone, I just need...help." Her voice faded. The smell of ammonia accompanied the creeping chill up my spine. What did any of this have to do with Crow?

"Since you seem so busy, don't let me distract you," Judy said, speaking of something I didn't understand. "I'll learn the rest by myself just fine. I'm a procurer of knowledge—"

"I thought you wanted to *practice* the magic," Senna said. "For spells to help the library's business pick back up."

Judy only shrugged with the look of irritation or pride or stubbornness across her pinched face. I couldn't tell what she was feeling, and I wasn't close enough to smell her emotions, but I could guess Senna had offended her. "I'll figure it out on my own. I know witches are the only ones who can cast intention magic, but anyone can learn a basic spell. Summoning or lighting a candle can't be that hard."

Senna merely shrugged and pulled a tube of Barbie-pink lipstick from her purse. "The difficulty depends on how much you practice."

Judy shot her daggers through narrowed eyes. I hopped to my feet before the Livid Librarian lost her cool and shoved the lipstick down Senna's throat. Or worse.

"Hey," Senna said as I approached, and her gaze slid to Judy before landing back on me. "Friend of Fate's right?"

"Me?" I pointed to myself, likely looking like a complete dolt in front of the witch whose help I needed and a highly-educated librarian. Not a good look for someone tracking a spell that was supposed to save the whole town from missing a once-in-a-decade tradition. "I never knew the guy. I was hoping *you* could tell me more about him. Or where the pages he stole ended up."

Senna's chin quivered and her eyes widened ever-so-slightly. "Look, I don't know what kind of game you're playing, but I don't know anything about the spell."

"Do you know anything about the guy who died trying it?" A new voice joined the argument, and all three of us nearly jumped out of our skin. Gemma and Sett stepped inside as the door swung shut behind them. Gemma smoothed back her slick, gelled ponytail and then rested her hands with her fingers around her brown belt. "And speaking of the spell, that book and any of its pages are evidence in an ongoing investigation."

Judy thrust a finger into the air and spoke with an air of

authority. "Actually, they're the official property of Bewitcher's Beach Library—"

Gemma raised her hand, palm facing Judy to cut her off. "Let me stop you right there. We're here for routine questioning, and I'd like to get down to business. It seems all three of you were seen near Fate's residence the night he was killed. I'll start with you, Judy."

They marched toward us, and Sett offered me a slight smile before his gaze dropped to the *evidence* in my arms.

Gemma turned to discuss the investigation with Judy while Senna slipped away, leaving the ripe stench of ammonia burning in her wake. The witch was clearly frightened, but she busied herself by running her fingers over the spines of stacked horror novels on a little table near the front desk. In front of the books was a sign that read *Dark Reads for a Long Winter: recommendations by Judy*. That wasn't ominous at all.

Sett passed by me and ran through some basic questions with Senna. The ammonia grew more sterile and stinky with every answer she gave him.

Ammonia. Fish.

Fear. Guilt.

"We were classmates." "No, not really friends." "Y-yes, I saw the spell he was working on."

At that, I spun around. Senna's wide eyes flicked to me, and she gnawed at her lower lip while her hands twisted the hem of her shirt.

"Do you have it?" I asked. "The protection spell?"

"Noema—"

I ignored Sett, keeping my focus on Senna.

"I—no." She squeezed her eyes shut and sighed. With the release of breath, the intense smells faded and were replaced by a hint of lavender, the calm scent that comes with telling the truth. "I don't have it."

It was as if the Drunken Oyster had come ashore, bringing with it the crash of waves that buried me under the weight of the sea. She didn't have the spell which meant my entire plan was set back and my heart was crushed. How could I give Stevie the holiday I'd promised without it? A pang struck my chest, and I sucked in a breath. "Do you know what happened to it?"

Senna shook her head. "Fate was practicing the magic, but I don't know where it is. I swear! And I didn't kill him."

"Thank you, Senna," Sett said. He turned and grabbed my arm. I expected a lecture for having interrupted him, but his voice—like his hold on my elbow—was gentle. "Did you smell anything? Was she lying?"

I shrugged. "She's definitely hiding something. But her emotions are all up and down. I can't pinpoint which one was a lie, except that she doesn't have the spell. Also, you should know, she seemed genuinely surprised when she saw Fate's body."

"Mayor Fitz has been pushing me to hurry this investigation up, so I appreciate your help." His gaze dropped to *The Book of Prophecies.* "We need to take the book down to the station."

After a moment's hesitation, I nodded and handed it to him. He leaned in, and the smell of freshly baked sourdough bread wafted from him. The scent matched no emotions, and it came strongly and clearly from Sett himself, not the grimoire.

He'd been baking again, but it'd been ages since he dropped by Mockbuster with homemade goodies. Maybe there were no leftovers with Gemma around. As frustrated as I was with him, it only took one touch, one whiff to feel comforted in his presence. Thoughts of the time he'd called himself my "backup" resurfaced. I'd never felt so safe. So...at home.

But now Gemma was in the picture, and he was busy being her backup. Or at least her police partner.

"Ms. Wolf!" Judy snapped. "What did I say about the growling?"

Again? All eyes were on me except Senna, who picked up a hardcover copy of *Dracula*. *Oops.* I cleared my throat and quieted the jealous rumble in my chest, tearing my attention away from the back of Gemma's head.

Sett's serious gaze shifted from me to Gemma. The tangy spice of pineapple pepperoni pizza emanated from his confusion. He blinked, and the smell faded as he leaned in, bringing with him the scent of sourdough again. The pups loved his homemade breads, pastas, and calzones almost as much as he seemed to enjoy joking around with the kids. But neither of us had time to nurture this friendship.

"Are you doing all right, Noema?"

"What? Yeah. I'm..." *Jealous of your new-old friend? Disappointed about the canceled holiday? Angry at you for being the one to encourage the cancellation? Worried about the safety of my friends and family in Bewitcher's Beach? You pick.* "Hungry," I said, finally. Hungry? That was what came out of my mouth?

Sett's flat lips quirked into a slight smile, and his eyes brightened. "Good thing I've got a loaf of sourdough with your name on it. As long as you set aside a bag of Orange Creme Savers for me before they sell out again."

My stomach grumbled, probably loud enough for the both of us to hear, and I returned the smile. "That's the best news I've heard all day. The kids refuse to eat grilled cheese unless it's made with slices of your sourdough. Honestly, you're ruining their perfectly good TV dinner palates. Before I know it, they'll be snubbing pizza bagels."

He chuckled and offered a playful cringe. "Sorry."

"Hey." I dropped my voice and stepped closer with my back turned to the three women. "I don't know how much you've looked into Judy yet as a suspect..."

"Judy?" he whispered as his brow wrinkled.

I nodded and explained my theory about the list of people who'd requested a look at *The Book of Prophecies*. The fact that Sett now held it in his arms as evidence to the investigation only further supported the thought. "Senna is the witch I saw at Fate's that night, but Judy tracks the books like a hound, plus she knew Fate from when he'd come here to study, *and* she's got a temper. I know she seems too small to grab him or push him into the wires, but she has that extra dragon strength from her ancestors."

Sett nodded, considering this.

Before he could respond, Gemma shouldered her way between us, absently nudging her splayed elbow into my side. She unhooked one thumb from her belt loop and snatched the grimoire from Sett. "That's enough meddling from a citizen. Isn't that right, Sheriff?"

A twinge fluttered in my stomach as Gemma leaned into Sett, their arms touching. The sneaky jealousy was back, and with it came an odor I was glad no one else could smell. Jealousy reeked of a skunk's attack that left my eyes stinging and watery.

Sett pursed his lips, glancing between us before he lingered on me. "I appreciate Noema's knowledge, and it is perfectly well within the law to consider information from witnesses with pertinent knowledge." He finally shifted to meet Gemma's intense gaze. "But you're right. Investigation policy doesn't include citizen sleuths."

To my surprise, Gemma smiled at me. "I'm sorry to break up the little partnership that I know you two had during a recent investigation, but let's keep this one professional. We're the ones who will find Fate's killer."

The oily, rancid smell of spoiling fish sloughed off of her as strongly as if she wanted me to know she was lying. She wasn't sorry about "breaking us up" at all. My stomach turned, souring so quickly that not even the promise of Sett's homemade bread could bring my appetite back.

I needed fresh air, and fast.

CHAPTER 10
PRETTY IN STINK

OUTSIDE THE LIBRARY, I swallowed an inadvertent growl and yanked the sweatshirt's hood over my head. The drifting, dark clouds hovered and threatened to further dampen my mood. Senna had slipped out of the library while Gemma's stinky guilt distracted me, and I was no closer to finding the pages. Not only did I miss my chance to request the witch's help, but Gemma had once again interrupted a friendly conversation between me and Sett.

I forced out a breath and shook like a wet dog, ridding myself of the irritation. Now that I knew Senna didn't have the spell, I wanted to look more closely at Fate and if he'd left any clues about who might have taken it. It was time to head back to the beachfront home and sniff around—just a bit.

I resisted the urge to drop into wolf form and run to the scene of the crime, remembering Hattie and I had a weekly tradition scheduled soon. Each week, we watched X-Files, swooned over David Duchovny, and bet whether or not Mulder and Scully would finally kiss. Maybe she'd agree to forego this week's episode and search for clues with me. It was worth a shot.

I DETOURED by Everland Theater and grabbed my best friend.

"We're going sleuthing?" Hattie folded her arms. "Well it's not as fun as debating non-existent tension between FBI agents, but count me in."

As we walked, Hattie interrogated me about my upcoming date with Crow. When her enthusiasm quickly deflated, I focused on finding the spell. If this didn't work, I'd be giving Senna another call. I sighed, biting back a howl at the heavy clouds suspended above the unruly waves. Once the new moon hit, our chance at seeing the ship on the shore was gone for another ten years.

We turned onto Beach Street, and I squinted at the sea, letting the rain soak my hoodie while I imagined a ghostly ship crashing over the violent waves. I could almost hear the creak of the wooden planks and the crackle of the bonfires meant to welcome the spirits. *Spirits that might be able to tell me who I am.*

With fat raindrops now splashing the cobblestone, I thanked my past self for staying free of the wet dog smell.

At the Kalabar home, the front gate was wrapped with yellow caution tape. I hopped over it and picked through the tall weeds, which were more of a deterrent than the police tape. If Gemma caught me here, she might demand Sett arrest me. Gemma was nice enough, but I couldn't shake her aggressive behavior and that awful smell that came from her guilt. Did she feel bad for getting in between mine and Sett's friendship? Or was it something worse? Why hadn't Gemma arrived at the scene of the crime with Sett?

Another spontaneous growl escaped me. I was simply jealous, and it needed to stop before I slipped up and suggested Sett arrest his new partner...and old girlfriend.

I glanced at the street, checking to be sure nobody was around before twisting the knob. It was locked. Unabashed, Hattie simply phased through the door and solidified enough to open it from the other side.

The door creaked open, and I scanned the scene. Not much had changed since I'd stumbled upon Fate's lifeless body. While Hattie headed up the grand staircase, I ducked into the study. The wires were still a tangled mess with a few on the table braided in a familiar pattern. Except this time electricity didn't buzz through them, which meant Fate's magic had officially faded.

"But everything else is the same," I said with a sigh. Apparently keeping the scene of the crime as untouched as possible was all part of the process. Or so I'd heard from Sett's stories. I straightened and ran my hand over the wires, the glimpse of the spell's woven pattern. "Were you trying to protect Bewitcher's Beach?" My whispered question was met with dead silence. Maybe if I knew more about Fate, I'd figure out who knew of his work with the protection spell. Was Senna only his classmate, or something more?

Something dropped through the ceiling like a glittering chandelier descending upon the center of the room. My heart leaped into my throat until I realized the "chandelier" was merely Hattie's golden dress. "There's nothing interesting upstairs that I can see," she said as if she hadn't just threatened a heart attack on me.

I blew out a breath. "Don't sneak up on me like that."

"What do you want me to do?" She folded her arms, sending the tassels on her dress vibrating. "Sing my way into the room?" Nostalgia and pride glazed in her faraway, unfocused eyes. "Actually, I'd rather like the reminder of my Vaudeville days before Hollywood stardom."

"Good. Then we agree that's a better idea than when you phase through the ceiling and almost make me pee my pants." I shuffled through the small space. The floorboards creaked like a ship riding the waves. Fate didn't have many personal items other than some clothes, a Kodak camera, a journal, and a huge collection of soda and cheap beer cans all stacked in a precarious tower. He seemed like a smart warlock, having gotten so far with a powerful and intricate spell, but this place looked and smelled like a frat house. "The only thing here is this notebook."

I thumbed through the journal, finding only sketches of...a trophy? A trophy with wings? I turned the page every which way and tried to make sense of it, landing on my original thought. The first drawing was a trophy that had grown bat's wings. The next pages showed a few sketches of people.

A familiar inky face beamed back at me from the page. Who had he drawn that I knew? Was it Senna's large eyes and thick lashes and the hint of a Mona Lisa smile? Though familiar, the drawing was artistic, rushed and smudged with ink. I couldn't quite place if it was the witch or not. I flipped to the back of the book and found scribbles I recognized. The sketches were drawings of the weaving pattern. I was sure of it. Warmth spread through my chest at the sight of the partial protection spell, and my lips parted with a whisper. "This is it." With vibrating hands, I turned to the next page, nearly ripping it, and found nothing but a blank page. "No!"

A jarring ring interrupted me, and I responded with a bark. My fingernails grew into claws but quickly retracted when I saw a blinking light on the heavy desktop. The sound rippled from an answering machine.

The Kalabar family's recorded message played, greeting the caller. It beeped once before another voice filled the room.

"Wassup my man?" A guy left an obnoxiously loud message. "Yo, Coach said to check in on you. Is that cop lady still questioning you? We're worried you won't make it back in time for the big game. Don't get yourself arrested, or Coach will be pissed. And tell Senna to hurry up with her half of the project. I need this spell to get me an A so I don't get kicked off the fly and field team. Later, man."

The dial beeped again. Cop lady? Why would Fate get arrested? "Do you think he was talking about Gemma?" I asked as I pointed to the answering machine. The logical answer was yes, considering Gemma was the only female cop in Bewitcher's Beach. My heart dropped, leaving a sickly weight in my stomach. Once again, Gemma appeared to be involved.

Hattie pursed her lips and narrowed her eyes at the machine as if it would give her the answer. Finally, she shook her head. "Honestly, Noema. I'm no investigator. If she knew Fate for some reason, Sett will find out."

"True." Sett was careful to follow every investigative policy, which meant he worked slowly. But it was also methodical and organized and led to uncovering the truth. I struggled to picture Gemma spending time around a frat guy like Fate, anyway. As much as the darker parts of myself wanted to blame her, she was guilty of nothing more than coming between the friendship I had with Sett. I tucked the notebook under my arm as we headed for the front door.

"So, are we thinking Senna lied about having the spell?" Hattie asked once we were outside, picking our way through the weeds and beer cans. Well, I was picking. Hattie was as elegant as ever, gliding through the grass and trash like a ghost queen.

"She said she didn't, but I smelled some guilt..." I'd been so sure Senna told the truth about the protection spell. The smell of guilt had to come from somewhere. But if her answer regarding the spell wasn't a lie, then her claim that she hadn't killed Fate must have been the source of the fishy stench.

I guess I was wrong. Dead wrong. "Doggone it!" I cursed, curling my hands until my wolf claws grew out and it hurt to make a fist.

Shivers stole through me as the wind picked up. A crack of lightning flashed behind the dark clouds, brightening the sky for a moment. Thunder followed, rumbling as if it agreed with my frustration. The sky's groan was distant now, leaving me with a dash of hope that the storm was on its way out of town. If Senna was a murderous criminal, then maybe we were back to square one as we waited for Madam Rowena to arrive—sooner now. The hopeful lift of my spirits didn't last.

Hattie arched a perfectly thin eyebrow. "Care to share your thoughts with the class?"

I sighed and explained that Sett needed to know about my mistake regarding Senna's source of guilt. Immediately.

CHAPTER 11
WITCHY BUSINESS

AS WE WALKED, I noted the absence of more pirate decorations. No longer did a miniature version of the Drunken Oyster adorn the front window of Scooby's Dog Grooming. Even the empty building by the firehouse had once had pirate stickers on the windows, decorated by neighborhood children. Those were now peeled off, leaving sticky residue in their absence. Was Bewitcher's Beach giving up on the Ghost Pirate Moon celebration already? The holidays were looking darker by the day.

The bright colors of the roller rink lifted my mood but only for a moment. It wasn't until I spotted Sett beneath the massive milkshake on wheels that I managed a smile. He stood outside Roller Shakes with his wings folded and his hands in the pockets of his navy police coat.

When Sett turned to us, his slate eyes sparkled and the crack of his stony cheeks split into a smile. "Just the woman I wanted to see—"

Before he could finish, Hattie cleared her throat loudly.

"I mean, the women I wanted to see." Sett corrected, flashing me an amused look. "I just meant, I've got a loaf of bread for Noema and the pups at my desk inside." He nodded his chin at the blue and gray police building that was wedged between Roller Shakes and the doctor's clinic. "I'll cook a beef stew to go with the grilled cheese sandwiches too. I know it's the pups' favorite, and I'd like to ask a favor of Stevie since she can speak with animals. I've got a pesky cat causing problems for some townspeople."

"You'd win Stevie over better with a batch of your famous surprise cookies."

"I thought you'd appreciate it if I stay away from extra sugar and provide a meal instead."

Sett was thinking of us? And of what I appreciated? He'd seemed so busy since Gemma came into town that it was hard to believe. Hattie sniffed again, eyeing us both now with her lips flattened and the edge of her high cheekbones sharpened. The sniffle was her not-so-subtle reminder that we'd tracked the sheriff down with a purpose. My stomach shriveled at the thought of giving up our one chance to cast the spell sooner rather than later. I sucked in a breath and dove into the explanation about the possibility of Senna's deadly crime.

"I'm so sorry I confused the smells. It's hard to narrow down exactly which feeling each scent is tied to when people are going through a range of emotions. Sometimes I can't even tell which person the smells are coming from."

"Noema." Sett gently touched my arm with his cool fingers, and my fiery wolf fever chilled for a moment. Was I rambling? Ugh. This was what Sett Lawrence did to me. Just his existence ramped me up. "There's no need to apologize. I appreciate your help, but I don't expect it to be hard evidence. Thank you for hurrying here with the information, but Senna has alibied out."

Hattie and I glanced at one another, mirroring an "o" expression before we blinked at Sett again and waited for more.

His muscular wings flickered. "Yeah. It was Noodle who

said he saw Senna outside Fate's after the coroner left that night, so we tracked her down to a small house in the woods out past the neighborhood. Gemma had seen her headed that way, so we stopped her, and Senna explained that she was at Chanel's boutique shopping for clothes at the time Fate was killed. Chanel and three of her customers confirmed this, and Senna even had a time-stamped receipt. She definitely didn't hurt her classmate."

I shook my head as my own emotions shuffled through an array of smells—confusion's pineapple pizza, smoky frustration, curiosity's mint, and then back to pineapple pizza. "Why was she acting so spooked when you questioned her then? I know I smelled guilt."

"And you were correct." He nodded. "Senna confessed that she knew Fate broke into the library and stole the protection spell for a project at Shadowvale University. After Fate started the spell, she realized it would be considered plagiarism and if the school found out, they'd all be expelled. She was too afraid to come forward because of that, and she thought she'd be considered an accomplice to Fate's breaking and entering. But since she alibied out for that too, she's cleared."

"Shopping again?" Hattie asked.

"Yep. Hopefully the kid doesn't go into debt hanging around Chanel's boutique." He tossed a thumb over his shoulder. "She's actually inside the station now giving her roommates a call to tell them she'll be stuck in Bewitcher's Beach for a few more days. I asked if she wouldn't mind checking in with Madam Rowena as well."

All at once, my muscles relaxed. Senna was someone I'd instantly felt connected to, and it was relief to know my mixed up smells had been wrong about her. She wasn't a killer but a friendly witch. *A witch who'd watched her classmate try to cast the spell.* If she remembered what he'd done, maybe she could recreate it before the Drunken Oyster appeared on the shore...

When she emerged from the station, Senna was beaming and cheerful despite the bad news about Madam Rowena's delay. The roads were still flooded, and the powerful witch professor didn't feel comfortable flying until the storm had officially moved on. I didn't blame her. As if on cue, the wind sped up again, whipping flags and banging the shutters on some of the smaller shops along the street.

"I know it's a lot to ask," I started, "but would you try the magic just to see if it works? We need the protection spell for an upcoming holiday."

She thought for a moment and then smiled. "I can write down what I remember and then work from there."

A thrill of hope rippled through me with a burst of energy.

She tugged a pink peacoat tightly across her chest as another gust swept through the streets and tossed wet leaves across the cobblestone. The coat bore Chanel's hand sewn label of an embroidered mermaid's tail below the collar's left fold. The breeze knocked her matching mermaid earrings against her cheeks. Evidence of her shopping was certainly obvious. "The weaving pattern is intricate. I can't promise anything, and it will definitely take me a few days to draw it up. And that's if I can get it right. I only stuck around Fate's house when we did homework, so I didn't exactly study his attempt very closely."

Like Mae had said, Senna wasn't friends with the frat boy. I thanked her about a dozen times before she finally laughed and said she had to get home. When we bid her goodbye, my heart soared. Everything was weaving together so nicely. Just like the spell itself would.

"When Noema gets this look, I worry," Hattie said, biting her lower lip.

Sett leaned closer to the ghost and rubbed his chin. "I'm with you on that. She looks like she has an idea."

"That's never good."

"Hey!" I shrieked and gave his bicep a friendly punch. "All I'm thinking about is how I still refuse to give up on the spell. *Somebody* took it, and I intend to find the original to restore *The Book of Prophecies* back to its former glory."

"Okay *Judy*, tell us more about this book obsession." Hattie's unamused voice matched her deadpan look.

I rolled my eyes. "What if Senna can't remember it?"

"Ah!" Hattie and Sett both spoke at the same time. They nodded and exchanged knowing looks.

"What? I want the spell for the book's glory and all that too, but we may as well keep looking for backup—" I clamped my jaw shut at the loaded word. Sett and I had once referred to one another as each other's "backup". The term was definitely more endearing and intimate than a friendly nickname, and we'd stopped saying it since Gemma had arrived and I'd started spending more time at Roller Shakes with Crow.

Sett's wings flickered and his eyes darkened for a moment, but he gave no other indication that the word triggered anything within him. I swallowed the gathered emotion through the tight squeeze in my throat. Was the storm ready to soak us again, or was that smell of rain coming from me?

"Let me walk you ladies home," Sett said. "Gemma will hold down the fort while I'm gone."

Thankfully, the wind relaxed as we made our way to the other end of town where Mockbuster and Everland Theater shared a corner with the local grocer. We harassed Sett for information on the murder investigation. When he waved us off, we talked about where else the spell could be and if Senna could recall the details in a timely manner. Hattie and I discussed theories of Judy's temper now that Fate's break-in was confirmed. Did the Livid Librarian lose it on the vandal? Sett shut our theory down, claiming there wasn't enough evidence against her.

Our little trio quickly turned to a duo when Hattie ditched us to hurry ahead. She disappeared through The Oyster Inn's wall of freshly-painted cream. The green trim was also new, having been updated before the storm hit. Barney and Hattie were an odd pair but were becoming fast friends. While he showed interest in the old films Hattie had starred in, she found fascination with the simplicity of his life of beige sweaters and plain toast. As a fairy, he also couldn't tell a lie, and my best friend appreciated all forms of blunt transparency.

I peeked through the window as we passed the inn. The grumpiest man alive was doing what I never thought possible. He smiled at Hattie, who performed the steps of a Vaudeville dance from her oldest glory days before Hollywood had made her a starlet on the screen.

Sett's wing grazed my arm, and a shiver rippled through me. "So," he began with a rough voice. He cleared his throat and continued, rubbing at the back of his neck as if feeling awkward. I couldn't smell anything peculiar, but I rarely caught Sett's scents. "I wanted to talk to you about Gemma."

"Talk? Gemma?" I folded back my ears in embarrassment then quickly pointed them upward again before he noticed. "I mean, there's nothing to say." *You can date whoever you want, even if she is a little snobby.*

He released a sigh. "She's new here, and I barely know her anymore. She's different from the person I knew back at the police academy."

"Oh?" I paused in front of Everland Theater to fix a fallen string of twinkling lights. Despite the storm's rage, the white lights still glowed brightly and made the old theater a little more inviting. The building desperately needed the updating that regularly treated The Oyster Inn, but we'd yet to put the money we'd earned from the fall festival into rebuilding. The cash was saved for an interior remodel that would change the stage into a big screen and bring a real movie theater to Bewitcher's Beach.

"Gemma needs a friend, and as her boss, policy dictates it's best if we don't have a close personal..." His voice faded. Relationship? Or friendship? I should have known Sett wouldn't cross a coworker line. He was the king of law and rules. Still, they often walked side-by-side too closely for mere work partners. "I was hoping you might find it in you to invite her to talk about movies. I've told her about your screenplays, and I know she's interested. It's right up her alley."

"Really?" I couldn't picture the sleek and focused cop interested in any form of art or media other than maybe...well, the show *Cops*.

"I'll send her to Mockbuster tomorrow if that sounds doable.'

I nodded, unable to find the words. Gemma wasn't exactly friendly like Senna, and I didn't love how she called me *Wolf* as if it was my first name.

"Will you do me a favor too?" I asked.

"Always."

Always. He said it as if nothing had changed between us. As if he was still my "backup." "Can I have Senna's address? I want to drop by her house and see what else she might know about *The Book of Prophecies*."

"Is this about the prophecy that mentions your particular skill? Hattie may have mentioned it to me." He knew me too well. I only shrugged and he continued. "Senna's place is tricky to get to so I'll have Gemma write up directions and bring it by tomorrow."

Another blast of wind rushed through the town, ringing the

windchimes that hung on the overhang at the grocery shop next door. The chill bit through my clothes, and I found myself leaning into Sett without thinking. As a wolf, I was usually overheated and appreciated the cool feel of Sett's skin whenever we stood close, but tonight's icy air had me wanting to huddle behind him to block the breeze.

When my unruly locks of wavy hair escaped the scrunchie that barely held them, Sett reached out and brushed a curl away from my face. Our eyes met and—for once—I smelled how he felt, and it was exactly what I was experiencing. Awkwardness.

He quickly pulled away and shoved his traitorous hand into his pocket.

I'd written him off after he'd arrested me only weeks before, and he could have lingering feelings for Gemma, all of which made this moment entirely inappropriate. Not to mention I had a date with Crow.

"I'll send Stevie down to grab the bread when you come back."

"Right."

With that, we parted ways, and I busied my mind with thoughts of tracking the spell. If neither Senna, Fate, nor Judy had it, who was left? And would Fate still be alive if he hadn't stolen it?

CHAPTER 12
ALL ABOUT GEMMA

A DAY OF TEDIOUS INVENTORY, waiting for Gemma, and no new information on the spell had me guzzling Diet Pepsi like it was hard liquor. Now I understood a pirate's affinity for rum. When the storm comes and the ship rocks too hard, it's tempting to drown yourself in liquid comfort. The bubbles and delicious syrup always settled my buzzing mind. Until the caffeine hit.

Methodically, I ticked off each VHS tape in the computer's recording system, double checking each box to confirm the correct movie belonged to the correct case. I found a few missing videos, a few cartoons swapped in the wrong cases, and somebody's home video in *Jurassic Park*'s box. This was typical for inventory, but the nervous fluttering in my stomach was not.

With each hour that past, critical time slipped away, and I had no idea where to look for the spell next. I munched a piece of popcorn from my afternoon snack and typed the missing *Jurassic Park* movie into the computer with a reminder to call the last renter and return their home video.

By the evening, I'd snagged a pack of Twizzlers from the candy display next to the register and enjoyed a snack while I worked, refusing to slow down even though the day was over. Gemma never showed up with the directions, but at least the absence spared me the awkward attempt of befriending a woman who wasn't my biggest fan.

Sitting cross-legged on the floor of the comedy aisle, I plucked VHS tapes off the shelf and scanned each one. Soon the stack of videos grew taller than my seated body.

"Why don't you hire more help?" Hattie phased through the new release wall and surged toward me.

"Can you read minds?" I asked. The ghost shook her head and pointed to the leaning tower of video cases that threatened to topple and bury me in a grave of B-movie comedies. Definitely not the way I wanted to go. I plucked the top video and returned each one to the bottom shelf before I stood. "Good point."

The bell above the door chimed, and Hattie's attention whipped to the front of the shop.

The familiar slick ponytail swung side-to-side as Gemma spotted us and marched past the first two rows. We greeted her halfway, and when we stumbled over words trying to immediately dive into small talk, I smelled her awkward embarrassment as a mixture of sour milk and tart yogurt. Apparently Sett had encouraged her to get to know me too considering she never spoke more than a few words to me at a time.

"So what do you like to watch?" Gemma asked.

I shrugged. "Everything. What about you?" The sourness wafted from me too. I almost dropped to all fours just to run away from this conversation. But Sett had requested my help inviting Gemma into Bewitcher's Beach, and if I was truly the friend of his that I claimed to be, I'd do him this favor. Besides, a warm chat between us would give me an opening to ask for directions to Senna's house without Gemma feeling as though I simply wanted something from her.

But warm it was not.

"Crime movies," she said with a sudden sigh. "So...Sett mentioned he'd like for us to be friendly." After an uncomfortable pause, she continued. "Look, we might have a few interests in common, but I really don't have the energy to do this. I'll just tell him we gave it our best shot and we'll stay cordial in case you'd like my expertise to improve one of your screenplays."

What was that supposed to mean?

Tension hardened in my jaw and muscles at the thought of Gemma lying to Sett. Before I could respond, the bell chimed, and we all turned to see a tall, dark, and cleaned-up Crow. His curls were gelled away from his face in a seductive swoop over his forehead. His normal black clothes were upgraded to a black button-down and slacks. He wore a sleek silver watch, but the face of the watch wasn't like anything I'd ever seen before. Rather than the twelve ticks of time, the device more closely resembled a compass with a hook-shaped arrow in the center. Pinched between his thumb and forefinger was a single red rose. A black ribbon decorated the thorny stem as if the flower was an extension of his outfit.

Heat burned in my cheeks when I tore my gaze away from the little gift and met his sparkling midnight eyes.

"I'm early. Should I come back?" he said, the perpetual smirk making its usual appearance.

"You should come *closer*." Hattie spoke under her breath without taking her eyes off of him.

His gaze flickered to Hattie and Gemma before it landed back on me. He extended his arm out, offering the rose. I wasn't one for flowers, but the thought still counted, and I graciously accepted. The fragrant rose was masked by the confusion as smells of pineapple pizza sloughed off of either Gemma or Crow. The scent shifted to a minty curiosity.

Gemma's eyes roved over us, and I jumped into action,

apologizing for the distraction. I assured Crow our date would start after I finished chatting with Gemma, and he easily agreed. He tilted his head to the left and backed away from us. "While you do that, I'll grab a bottle of wine from next door."

As we watched him leave, I summoned the courage to try a little harder with Gemma. She was a tough case to crack, but I'd made a promise to Sett and I wasn't going to lie to him that we'd given friendship a try. "If you don't have the energy then let me get you a snack and we can start with something simple. Where did you move from?"

She shook her head, pony tail swishing. "No." The statement didn't match her unusually cheerful voice and the odd smile that ghosted her face. "I want to know about *you*. Forgive my earlier suggestion. I'm feeling better now and would like to try this again. I was simply tired after dealing with a suspect this afternoon."

I exchanged a glance with Hattie. "A suspect? Was it Judy?" I ventured a guess.

Gemma pinched the bridge of her nose and then plastered on a tight smile. "You really are rather smart, Noema." The unexpected compliment confirmed my suspicion, and a shiver tickled my neck. Judy killed Fate. Or at least the cops had reason to believe so.

The conversation was quickly swept away from the murder investigation. Before I knew it, I was enjoying my last bite of a Twizzler rope when Gemma insisted I tell her the top three movies I loved the most.

I shoved the candy wrapper into my jeans pocket and wiped my hands. "Only three? That's a really tough question. I can pick three from any one genre but three overall? Hmm." I took a moment to think while Gemma stared at me, unblinking. "*The Princess Bride* because it has the perfect balance of comedy, drama, and adventure. *The Lion King* because it's simply a masterpiece. And *The Breakfast Club* because even though the characters are all so different, they become like a little family for a while."

"And you're a fan of Twizzlers, I see," she said. "I'm a Snickers gal myself."

"Ah, chocolate." I shrugged. "I'm allergic."

Gemma burst into a hearty laugh, patting her chest to calm her after a moment. "Right, right. Because you're canine."

"Werewolf," I specified.

"Does that mean you enjoy playing catch...or fetch?"

"She *is* the resident soccer mom," Hattie interjected.

I rolled my eyes, but she wasn't wrong. "I like soccer and running and writing too, of course, especially mysteries. With a cold Diet Pepsi in hand. But enough about me; what do you do for fun?"

Gemma smoothed imaginary flyaways back with her palm and straightened. "Fun? Well, I'm *accomplished* in many areas. One of those being acting from before I was a cop. Speaking of, I'd like a role in your newest work."

My ears perked. "Definitely, but first I wanted to ask about Senna. Sett said you'd give me her address so I can speak with her about the grimoire."

"The grimoire?"

I nodded and explained Senna's plan to attempt to recreate the protection spell from memory.

Her brow quirked before she pursed her lips. The look was immaculate on her perfectly proportioned face. The curve of her eyeliner and the slight tint of pink on her lips and cheeks revealed her skill with makeup. It enhanced her natural beauty without being too heavy. As much as I'd wanted to dislike her, she made it impossible now. Gemma and I were too much alike, enjoying favorites such as *Clue, The X-Files,* and *Law and Order.* Or so she claimed with each favorite show I mentioned. "Is Senna working with the other warlock?" she asked.

"What other warlock?"

Gemma waved the question away and finally nodded. "Never mind. Contact us if she gets close to accomplishing the spell. It could help us understand Fate better." She dug into her coat pocket and produced a slip of paper. "This is the address. Be careful."

I accepted the paper with a firm nod. "Thank you, and I won't get in the way of the investigations anymore."

"See that you don't." She flicked her ponytail as if ridding her face of hair, but not a single flyaway plagued her. With a lift of her chin, she looked down at me, and I realized her ankle boots put her a few inches taller than me. "Now, about a role for me. What kind of mystery are you currently working on?"

After retrieving my spiral-bound notebook, I showed Gemma the screenplay's first page that I'd only barely begun scribbling. The outline covered the basics. The story was about a woman who swerved to avoid hitting a cat in the road and crashed her car into a murderer's house, only to discover she saved a second victim's life right before the killer acted. When I revealed that the cat was a shapeshifter girl who was saving her father's life, Gemma's smile twisted to a frown.

She ran her tongue along her top teeth and huffed. "Well, I can look young but I certainly wouldn't play an animal."

"Shapeshifter," I corrected.

With a wave of her hand, she dismissed me. The flare of her nostrils and the odors of anger and fear didn't match her casual gesture. "I don't like the car—" she swallowed hard. "Accident idea either."

Hattie cocked her head. "You could play the murderer."

Gemma forced a smile. "I'll wait for you to add another character. Perhaps a skilled detective who tracks the killer."

"I don't plan—"

"Good luck," she said with a spin. The tip of her ponytail whacked me in the nose and sparked a sneeze. Gemma stepped over another tower of inventory I'd left unfinished and made her way to the door, still with my notebook in her hand. She opened the door as a shapeshifter family walked through, coming to rent a comedy, no doubt. Noodle waddled inside after his dad, carrying a lollipop in one tentacle. With a tight smile, Gemma ducked outside.

"But you have my notebook." My voice died in my throat. Maybe she wanted to use the outline I'd written to prepare for the screenplay. At least it'd give me a good excuse to buy a fresh pack of notebooks.

A high-pitched gasp that nearly shattered the windows erupted from Hattie. She thrust a transparent finger in the air. "That's where I know her from!"

Noodle stared up at the ghost with shining eyes before erupting into tears, surprised by Hattie's outburst. His father guided him away from the ghost.

After apologizing to the customers for my friend, I turned to Hattie. "What are you talking about?"

"Gemma is Gemma Stone. The actress!" she said. "I recognize her from that Lifetime movie. She's the actress whose parents died in a hit and run. I remember seeing it on the news. No wonder she didn't like the car accident plot."

"Gemma Stone," I repeated, trying to place her face on the screen. But she was too good with makeup, and since some characters looked wildly different from the actor's normal self, it didn't help. "Huh. I should have realized. Sett told me she's an actress. Or she was before she quit and turned to law and order. Apparently there's nothing she can't do."

"Poor doll. I can't imagine so much grief." She gasped again, and the little shapeshifter octopus yelped from two aisles away. The father popped his head over one of the aisles to give Hattie another glare. After mouthing an apology, Hattie lowered her voice. "I bet that's why Gemma moved here. To get a fresh start after the tragedy. It's the same reason Bette and I didn't choose to haunt Hollywood after the fire."

"Right." I glanced toward the door, though I could no longer spot Gemma outside in the dark street. "And Sett can comfort her." A twinge of sadness skipped in my heart. After all the irritation I'd harbored toward her, guilt flooded me. I'd been so jealous of Gemma that I wanted to blame her for the murder. But now our similarities struck me; we shared a familiar heartbreak—a lonely life after the loss of family.

CHAPTER 13
ROMANCING THE WOLF

AFTER THROWING HALF my curls into a ponytail, I
headed back down to the shop knowing Crow would be back
any minute. I tightened the scrunchie at the crown of my head
and hopped down the staircase two steps at a time, smoothing
the fresh hoodie I'd thrown on over an ankle-length navy blue
dress with tiny white flowers.

I retrieved *Alien Resurrection* and readied the TV for the
night.

When Crow arrived, we sat side-by-side, watching the TV
I'd dragged out of storage and intended to hang on Mockbuster's wall, the same way Roller Shakes mounted their
screens and played videos all day. For now, I'd propped it on
the desk between the computer register and a VCR. The
screen flashed with dark images of the menacing alien species,
and Squeaks' eyes darted from Sir Crabby to Crow and finally
to the creature on the TV.

He released a faint whimper, and I leaned forward in my
stool, scooping him into my hands. "It's all right."

"Too much for the little guy?" Crow asked, shifting his gaze
from Squeaks to me. The mouse's whimper lowered to a grunt

as his tail whipped with aggressive flicks that curled and slapped the back of my hand. Crow's eyebrows lifted, and he crooked a smile. "I didn't mean to offend."

"Too late." I cringed. "Squeaks is *particular* with new... friends. It probably doesn't help that the villain of his story seems rather taken with you."

Sir Crabby's many legs carried him sideways until he came out from under the chair and clamped a claw around the hem of Crow's pants.

"Villain, huh?" Crow twisted to reach for the crab. With some effort, he pried the claw from his pant leg and set Sir Crabby in his lap. After a moment, Sir Crabby splayed his legs out, flattening against Crow's legs, and then tucked his claws in close. A smirk and a breath through his nose indicated Crow's approval of the crab's interest in him. "We understand each other."

With the conversation started, I angled my knees toward Crow and let the movie play in the background, silently swearing I'd let him rent a copy of the new release for free. "Hey so I know he was kind of a nuisance at the roller rink, but do you happen to know much about Fate's life? If Senna can't recreate the spell, I was hoping to figure out who might have taken the pages from Fate."

Crow pursed his lips, squinting at a scene with Sigourney Weaver and Winona Ryder on the screen. Finally, he blinked at me and shrugged. "I really don't know him." The lack of the guilty rotten fish odor told me he spoke the truth. I had to get more specific. What else had he overhead from Fate and Senna's argument?

I opened my mouth to ask more, but a chime interrupted me. We both twisted to see a hulking figure step through Mockbuster's door. Thick wings folded tightly to Sett's broad shoulders. He ducked into the shop and paused at the sight of us staring at him.

His slate eyes shifted from me to Crow and finally to the TV on the desk in front of us, and his lips curved into a frown. The actress's scream split through the momentary silence when a horrifying alien attacked her.

"Noema." Sett dipped his chin in a slight nod. "Crow."

Squeaks chirped until the sheriff's gaze dropped to my hands.

"Squeaks," he said, appeasing the little mouse before forcing a tense smile in my general direction. Clearing his throat, Sett pointed to the TV, and his wavering attempt at a smile quickly dropped to a grimace. "I see the next *Alien* movie is out."

"Yep, uh, yeah," I said. *Of course! I should have told Sett his most awaited release was here.* I took a sip of soda to ease my dry mouth. Not even the comforting flavor of Diet Pepsi kept my stomach from flipping again. The awful odor of my own guilt had my nose wrinkling as my cheeks burned. Thankfully, nobody else could smell emotions.

Crow looked between us, entirely unbothered. "It's fantastic so far. If you're a horror buff, you've got to rent it."

Oh curses. Don't call it a horror in front of Sett. I cringed and held my breath for a moment of reprieve from the thick air.

"You mean science fiction," Sett said, staring at Crow with all the intensity of an officer witnessing a crime.

Crow half-smiled. "Excuse me?"

Before a debate on the *Alien* franchise's genre broke out, I shot to my feet and interjected. "Technically, it's both science fiction and horror."

With a sigh, Sett tilted his head to the door. "Can I have a word? It'll just take a moment from your...date."

I squeezed my eyes shut and let the awkwardness wash over me like a wave crashing down from the shore. Unfortunately, I wasn't in wolf form and couldn't run from this triple-decker sandwich of ingredients that didn't fit: a werewolf, a human, and a gargoyle.

I glanced at Crow, and he straightened, scooting back in his chair to let me pass by without having to climb over his legs. The door swung shut behind me, and Sett turned, wings nearly whacking me as he moved faster than usual.

"Really, I didn't mean to interrupt your..." he trailed.

Seriously? Don't say it again. This is too weird.

His wings flicked, expanding and then settling closer to him in a shrug as he finally met my gaze. "So I wanted to thank you. Gemma was in the best mood I've seen in a long time. Positivity really goes a long way in our line of work."

"Good. I'm glad. Any chance there's positive news on risking the holiday even if Senna doesn't cast the spell?" I figured now was as good as any to prod him about it, just in case the witch wasn't up to the task and Madam Rowena still refused to fly to Bewitcher's Beach.

He shook his head. "Unfortunately, I just cannot allow it now that there's another threat in town."

"Doesn't Mayor Fitz want it to happen? And what about the vote?"

"He wants it, yes. But he wants his people safe more and he defaults to me for that."

A low growl built in my chest at the memory of the disappointed faces, Cordelia's frown, Hattie rolling her eyes—but the one that hurt the most was Stevie's sobs.

"I'm sorry about the holiday." He sucked in a breath and continued. "Spending more time with you and the pups...it got me thinking about how I wasn't doing enough for the families in Bewitcher's Beach."

"So you'll cancel a family holiday...for the families?" I arched an eyebrow.

"Noema—"

"Sett." I leveled with him, keeping my gaze steady. Maybe suppressing my irritation with his rash decision wasn't the best choice. It bubbled now, ready to spill out between my bared teeth. "You saw what people wanted; they can make the decision to stay home and not participate if a few of the ghosts have turned to poltergeists. You can try to protect the town, but canceling a tradition isn't the way to do it. You're breaking people's hearts, and it isn't fair to go to the extreme just to convince yourself you've done a thorough job protecting everyone—"

"Protecting you!" His hands shot out and grabbed my arms, cutting my rant short. Despite his rough skin and firm grip, a gentle, sweet scent filled the minimal space between us. He released me and regained his stoic composure with a glance everywhere that wasn't my face. "I just mean that protecting the residents here has been more personal for me, and I might have jumped too quickly to the safest and most disappointing option. Maybe even unnecessary if..." He gestured generally at me with one hand and lifted his other to scratch the back of his neck before he found my gaze again.

The pleasant, enticing aroma grew thicker. *Vanilla.* I'd smelled it when Mae and her husband Wallace teased one another. I'd smelled it whenever Cordelia spoke of her boyfriend Roman. I'd smelled the scent of love for the first time years ago, when Christopher kissed me on our first date and with every kiss after that until he passed. Of course Sett loved me—as a good friend and a helpful Bewitched citizen.

"If Senna can do it." I finished the sentence for him.

"Or we can set up summoning diamonds to prepare for poltergeists. There are other options."

"Ghost traps?" I asked, referring to the difference between summoning circles and summoning diamonds. A diamond could trap anyone summoned within, not just an angry spirit. "So this means you and Fitz will go ahead with the invitation?"

He sighed. "Only if we have time to prepare, and this investigation is soaking every spare moment so far. Like I said, with a murderer at large, I can't spread myself too thin. But if the case gets settled well before the new moon, we can work on gathering the pirates' favorite items to summon any poltergeists. It will be a lot of prep work since summoning items must be personal."

"When did you learn so much about summoning?"

"When I found out Fate had his favorite items missing from his house. Senna clued me in and suggested someone might have been preparing to summon him, which, if it was a diamond trap, could be sinister."

"I could help!" It slipped out, natural, sudden, and with thoughts of the last case we'd solved together buzzing in the air between us. "I've been reading a lot about spells, summoning included, in *The Book of Prophecies*."

To my surprise, he took a step closer to me, mere inches from my face. Even his chilly, stony skin couldn't cool the heat burning my chest and cheeks and neck. Several smells rolled off of him. Vanilla mixed with confidence's earthy sandalwood, minty curiosity, and a hint of lavender. "You'll help by finding that spell."

I nodded, not wanting to break the current *spell* between us. The moment of heavenly smells was almost as good as the scents I found between the grimoire's pages. Maybe better since these didn't come with confusing delusions and daydreams.

"I'd offer my aid if I had time, but this case has been tricky." He blew out a breath. "Anyway, I've been keeping an eye on

Judy since you mentioned it. I caught her in a lie that she'd never seen Senna except for as a library patron."

"How do you know?"

"Mae told me," he said with a smile. "She'd gossiped to half the town that the new witch and the librarian snubbed her dog when she was at the park for a walk. I guess they didn't want to pet her poodle, and Mae was personally offended."

I laughed. "Sounds like her."

"When we questioned Senna, she had no trouble sharing the truth that she's been helping Judy learn witch history, but she didn't know what for. I dug a little deeper on Judy and found out she's threatened Fate before when he forgot to return a book. She even tracked him down at his house to get it. It's certainly suspicious, but we're still waiting on fingerprints from the crime scene. If they match Judy, this case should be closed before the new moon." Sett's gaze flicked to behind me, likely scrutinizing my dark and handsome date through the window. A frown pulled at his mouth, signaling a change in the conversation and a sudden shift in his mood. Gingerly, he cupped my elbow and I uncrossed my arms. "I promise I'm not trying to cross a line." My breath caught, mistaking his reach as going to hold my hand, but he pulled back and eyed the scene inside Mockbuster again. "Be careful with Crow, Noema."

Where did that come from? Was Sett jealous or merely his usual overprotective self?

"Gemma had heard of him before they both came to Bewitcher's Beach. Apparently, he harbors some secrets."

I narrowed my eyes. Didn't we all? Not everybody knew I could smell emotions, but did that make my peculiar talent a secret? I had no reason to believe whatever Gemma claimed about Crow. She didn't even know him, and it seemed this only served to rile Sett's need to be protective. "What kind of secrets?"

"I'm not sure. Gemma said he's always moving like he's on the run." Sett's jaw tightened. There were plenty of reasons people relocated frequently, and many were not nefarious. I'd been there once, searching for a safe haven to raise my werewolf pups."I know this is coming at an awkward time, but Crow tried to report someone stalking him and when Gemma looked into it, there was no evidence. Just a strange claim from a guy who won't tell anyone his last name. It didn't add up, and I couldn't bear it if you got hurt." He swallowed hard. I wasn't going to get hurt from Crow, but Sett was doing a darn good job of hurting me with the canceled holiday threats. And now this?

I lifted my chin in defiance, trying to level his gaze though he stood a few inches taller than me. "I don't have a real last name either. Do people need to be careful around me?"

He knew exactly what I meant by that. He knew I carried the guilt of Christopher's death because life as a werewolf wasn't always safe. He knew I'd sworn off soulmates because I'd lost my first love when I wasn't careful enough.

Sett's eyes squeezed shut for a moment. "Noema, that's not what I meant."

I didn't respond.

"I'm sorry. I'll leave you to it." With that, Sett turned and strode toward the town square.

The door flew open behind me, and Crow barrelled through.

"Thank you for the viewing," he said, breathless. As he stepped in front of me, another whiff of birch with a hint of decay tickled my nose. Confusion and a dash of fear raised goosebumps on my arms. For a moment, we stared at one another as I held back a cough. The decaying scent was suddenly so strong and my stomach turned. He reached out and pinched a curl that had escaped my scrunchie and tucked it behind my ear. "I'll be back to finish that movie another night."

"Is something wrong?"

"I'm sorry. I have to go." He turned and, like Sett, strode away without another word. *Unlike* the gargoyle, he moved twice as fast, already several yards away from me in a few steps. This night was a whirlwind of emotions, but I tried to block out the myriad of smells swirling from my anger and sadness and confusion.

Did Sett's interruption bother Crow? Or was there an emergency at Roller Shakes? But he didn't head the direction of the roller rink, instead walking with his sights set on Chanel's boutique. Who went shopping at this time of night? And suddenly? I sucked in a breath and suppressed the questions swirling in my head. None of the speculations explained the strange smell buried beneath his emotions.

The smell of decay. And death.

CHAPTER 14
HATTIE AND NOEMA'S EXCELLENT ADVENTURE

THE NEXT DAY was full of inventory, another pack of Twizzlers, and reading with Dio, who struggled to finish his homework. Hours flew by, ticking closer to the time Hattie and I planned to pay Senna a visit. Once the kids settled in for the night with Bette as their babysitter, we took to the cobblestone streets.

Outside, the calm, unending storm showered us. I let it wash away last night's lingering unease from Sett's visit and my date with Crow. Tonight was a new adventure. The delicious scent of banana cream pie revealed my excitement to see how far Senna had come on the protection spell.

We turned into the neighborhood where the houses blocked some of the sea wind. The trip through the suburbs only furthered my resolve to find the pages and reinstate the holiday. Pirate flags hung on houses, billowing in the wind, while twinkling white lights trimmed gutters and fences. Wire ships were mounted on green lawns, and banners decorated garage doors that read *Welcome Spirits* or *Greetings Ghosts* or *Happy Swashbuckler Celebration!*

Finally, we made it to the far corner of the neighborhood

where the houses were spread thin and the suburbs no longer existed with paved roads and concrete driveways. A dirt path led to more rural residents on the edge of town, bordering wine country to the south. Nothing but hills and trees and vineyards in the distance could be seen for miles around on this side of Bewitcher's Beach.

Gravel crunched beneath my sneakers as Hattie silently surged ahead to check the address on the next gate. Shadows danced across the dirt at my feet and the wind rustled through the trees. Long branches hung down in the road and criss-crossed overhead for a canopy of nature's arms reaching as if in an embrace. The trees had lost their leaves a month before, now with bare cragged branches that housed hooting owls and a curious crow that cocked its head at me. Was that Senna's animal familiar? I knew some witches had them. The tattooed wings popped into my mind's eye, and I squinted at the trees, trying to spot a bat.

"Two hundred," Hattie said as she floated back toward me. "And the mailbox said two hundred and two."

Then where's 201? The space between the spread-out properties was a grove of trees with no fencing, no mailbox, and what may have been a driveway, now overgrown and barely visible. We exchanged a glance and turned down the winding path of wild growth and trees.

Hattie hurried ahead, phasing straight through tree trunks and spiked berry bushes. "It's a dead end," she said once I caught up.

I picked through weeds and stopped beside her where she looked at a wire fence that bordered the vineyard. Had we walked that far? One more step and we'd be out of Bewitcher's Beach boundaries.

"There!" Hattie pointed, her arm going right through my nose. When I turned, she was already darting toward a small building. "Look at us." She laughed. "We're quite the sleuthing sisters these days." While Hattie's reference to me as her family member warmed me, the sight of the run-down cottage had the opposite effect. The old house seemed straight out of a book of fairy tales where an evil woman might lead children into a cooking cauldron. I frowned and followed the ghost to the haunted-looking hut.

Vines had grown over the walls, nearly covering the entirety of the gnarled wood panels. Dozens of pots lined the little porch, each housing thorned ivy plants. The saucer of one potted planter was left abandoned without its accompanying pot. The steps creaked underfoot, and with Hattie's nodding encouragement, I lifted my fist to knock.

No answer.

After several knocks, Hattie lost her patience and thrust her head through the door. I'd been working to temper my impulsiveness, but all the resistance melted, and I begged her to tell me what she saw.

"Nobody is home, and something looks off," she said. That was enough for me. I grabbed the handle and twisted, pushing through the unlocked door.

The space was small where a round table sat in the center. A bed took the length of the back wall except for a door that was open to a bathroom. On the right, a small kitchen was left dirty with a crusty pan of leftover Kraft mac and cheese.

Among the mess, double doors were splayed open, revealing an immaculate closet. Each fashionable item hung on a rack or was neatly folded on a shelf and arranged by color. The only thing out of place was an abandoned hanger on the floor, one that had snapped at the neck and would no longer work to hook onto the rack. This didn't seem like the house of the witch in the coordinated outfits. Something was amiss.

Hattie pointed at a pile of books dumped in a heap by the

head of the bed. I shuffled across the space and carefully thumbed through each one, looking for any notes on the spell tucked beneath the Harlequin romances. Little scribbles annotated the pages in tiny, neat lettering with notes that read: *this is where she falls for him* and *why can't this guy be real?* Senna was a bookworm, which made sense now why she and Judy seemed like friends. I replaced the novel on the stack and looked over the bed. A lone bookmark sat by the pillow on the wrinkled sheets. It seemed she'd taken the book she was currently reading with her. I set down the book with a cover of an embracing couple on the mattress and plucked the bookmark off the sheets.

The laminated piece of paper looked cut straight out of Fate's sketchbook with the same image of a trophy. Was this the reward Fate was after? Who would grant them this trophy and for what? Recreating the spell?

"Noema." Hattie interrupted my thoughts. I returned the bookmark and swiveled to see the ghost hovering over the round table.

Tacked into the wood fluttered a piece of paper. It was whipped about by a gust of wind that blew through the open door.

The crease on Hattie's brow inspired me to hurry across the length of the house. A chill spread goosebumps over my neck and shoulders as I caught sight of the scribbled writing.

I scanned the note, and my blood ran cold.

I can't do the spell. So stop sniffing around, stop calling me, and don't you dare look for me. ~Senna.

My knees went weak, and I suddenly wished I was balanced on all fours. The stench of my own fear grew thick. "Is–is this meant for me?" How many times had I called her, desperate to get her to try the spell? And the sniffing comment...that was definitely directed at me. Had I offended

Senna? *No.* "Wait." I froze, finally identifying what looked off about the creepy note. This handwriting didn't match Senna's annotations. I quickly retrieved the Harlequin novel and put the words side-by-side to show Hattie.

Sparkles from the flapper dress bounced around the room as the ghost gave herself a little wiggle. "Yikes, this certainly wasn't written by Senna and it looks like she left in a rush. This place is a disaster."

"We have to tell Sett," I said, tearing my eyes away from the note. "The killer came after Fate when he was working on the protection spell, and when Senna did the same, she went missing. That can't be a coincidence." It was my idea, my request, my plan to have her recreate the spell's pattern that might now get the young witch murdered. Nearly buckling at the knees, I steadied myself with a hand on the table. My pulse thrashed in my ears.

Judy was their main suspect. Had she found out about Senna's confession—that Senna knew about Fate's break-in and the damage to the library? Judy also knew I was actively looking for Senna which would have clued her in that I'd come here. But Fate's death seemed a crime of angry passion. Did Judy have the cold-blooded heart for premeditated murder?

I couldn't wait around speculating when the young witch's life was on the line.

Claws extended from my nails and sliced through the corner of the threatening note still pinched between my fingers. Fur replaced the clothes that slipped off of me as I dropped to all fours and bolted for the door.

With a howl that echoed through the grove of trees and into the night, I ran, and the ghost followed in my wake. The sheriff needed this information faster than two legs could carry me.

Before the killer had a chance to hurt anyone else.

CHAPTER 15
THE UNUSUAL SUSPECTS

ON MY HIND legs and with my forepaws stretched up, I reached the height of the station's doors. I scratched at the crack between the door and the frame and whined, waiting for Hattie to reappear from the other side of the wall. After a moment, the ghost phased through the locked door with a frown.

"They're not here," she said.

I barked in understanding and dropped with all four paws to the cobblestone.

Follow me! Across town we hurried, loping down the street through the dense fog that had rolled in off the shore. The same fog that always coated the town this time of year. The same fog that made it impossible for the Drunken Oyster ship to find the shore and allow the ghosts to come mingle with friends and ancestors.

If Judy returned to the library for a show of normalcy, hopefully Sett was there too. Ammonia burned my nose, and a sneeze overcame me. The odor of my own fear and worry for the witch hung in the air around me.

Moisture clung to my fur coat with a heavy dampness over

my back and head. I slowed to double-check Hattie still followed me as I padded over the beach's sandy walkway to the library on the other side. In the mist, I could barely make out Hattie's glow. Her thin, transparent frame blended with the cloud of gray.

Before I twisted my neck to look where I was going, I slammed into something solid. Something stony.

I allowed myself to breathe through the shock and the ache in my shoulder where I'd slammed into Sett. Sett's butt, anyway.

Heat rippled through me as I tucked my tail and backed away from where his slacks hugged his muscular legs and butt. A mixture of embarrassment, worry for Senna, and relief flooded me.

The police car was parked sideways with one tire on the walkway. He'd arrived here in a hurry.

I barked and howled and skipped on my front paws but it was Hattie he looked at. In a rush of words tumbling over one another, she explained the note at Senna's and my theory about Judy.

Sett nodded. "Gemma said an anonymous witness called with a tip. They confirmed that Judy was seen at Fate's the evening he was killed. I'm here to take her in for another round of more in-depth questions." With that, he turned and yanked the library's door open. He ducked inside and folded his wings tightly. "Judy!" he called in a deep reverberating yell. I bounded in after him before the heavy door swung shut.

In a flash of red hair, the librarian emerged from the aisle marked *history* with her arms full of books heaped haphazardly on top of one another. Freckles dipped into the creases across her forehead, between her brows, and lining the frown around her mouth. Her floor-length pioneer skirt tangled around her legs as the hem dusted the floor.

Judy released an exasperated huff. "I'm so glad you're here. Senna was taken." She stumbled toward the front desk, nearly tripping over the thick fabric as she let the books fall from her hold. Some splayed open, others smacked hard spines against the desktop, and still more tumbled to the floor. Everything about her behavior was wrong. Judy never treated sacred books like this.

Sett's brow furrowed. "Where is she?"

"She. Was. Kidnapped." Judy growled, pinching the fingers of both hands together as if holding a string taut in front of her. Impatience mixed with irritation in a suffocating smoky scent. The odor tightened my throat, leaving me breathless and panting.

All at once, the suffocating stench subsided, giving away to ammonia as she noticed me. The librarian's gaze slid behind Sett to where I stood, my head entirely too close to his...butt. I skipped to the side, and her eyes followed me, wide and panicky, She wagged a finger at me, mouth open. For once, Judy didn't have a snide remark to send my way, instead at a loss for words.

Sett glanced at me, tucking the bottom tip of his massive wing closer to his leg to see me at his side. Fur raised across my back, and a growl rumbled in my belly.

"Arrest her," Judy finally breathed, still pointing at me. "She's the one who kidnapped Senna!" Without taking her eyes from me, she felt for a book on the desk, grabbing the closest one and holding it high beside her head as if ready to throw it at me.

Sett stepped forward, putting himself between us. "Judy, let me have the book."

She yanked it from his reach and backed away, edging around the desk. "I have proof that Noema requested *The Book of Prophecies* in my records many times. She was tracking Fate and Senna. Now they're both gone."

I barked. *I was tracking the spell!*

"Judy, let's do this the easy way," Sett said. "My partner just radioed to me to confirm that Miss James is not at her house, and it's clear Noema is not with her right now. You can tell me what makes you think Senna was kidnapped when I bring you down to the station."

After a moment's hesitation, she lowered the book. "Absolutely not. I know you and Noema are friends, and she's probably trying to frame me!" She pointed at her own bared teeth and then at me. "I will not be bitten by a rabid dog—"

"Miss Knovel!" Sett shouted, startling all three of us to stand a little straighter. My tail lifted at attention. Before speaking again, Sett settled himself with a slow breath. "Please." He held out his open palm to a chair at the round table in the center of the library.

Judy took a seat, but not without keeping a close eye on me the entire time. With her anger and accusations temporarily squelched, the shaking in her fingers and pungent fear caught my attention and then descended into the fishy odor of guilt. "I should have called you, but I was in shock, and then I realized what might have happened to her. Senna disappeared," she said, her voice quivering now as her eyes grew wide and glassy. She pointed to the desk. "She was standing right there, talking about the protection spell one moment, and then she was gone."

The protection spell? My ears perked, extending long and pointed where they came together on the top of my head. This was more proof that Senna's connection to recreating the spell was also likely her demise—the target on her head for the killer. Killers like Judy...

"And why do you say that was a kidnapping?" Sett asked.

The librarian palmed her face and sighed as if Sett was an annoying child who didn't listen and therefore didn't understand the obvious. "Because that's what Senna said!" She let her arms fall from where she touched her temples and slam against the tabletop. Her gaze ping-ponged between the three of us. "She literally said 'I'm being taken.' Then there was glowing around her, and she screamed—" Her voice caught in her throat, and she gingerly touched her chest. "She screamed that she was being kidnapped. Then *poof!*" Finally, she buried her face in her hands, and the awful oily fish odor rose again. Judy was feeling guilty. This whole story must be a lie. A deflection.

My gaze fell to the books Judy had dropped by the desk. In the pile of witch lore and historical records, two books didn't match. One was a harlequin romance with a cowboy passionately kissing a woman in a full-length dress. The cover of the other book read *The Planting and Caring of Thorned Ivy.*

My mind raced, recalling the mess in Senna's home. She'd been reading a romance in this same series and had a missing thorned ivy plant from her front porch. I padded to the desk and sniffed at the books on the floor. After digging and carefully pawing at the spine of a book, it tumbled off the pile, revealing another title that didn't match the historical texts and records. Even more odd, the book wasn't a book at all but a magazine. *Sorcery and Style.* A shimmering, tanned woman beamed up at me from the cover among the black, brown, and blue books that surrounded it.

Little phrases decorated the magazine with exclamation points and in bold font. *Fashionable crystals! Dress to impress for under $100. New styles for old traditions: holiday wear to WOW!*

I barked and Judy yelped. Another bark and Hattie surged forward. "What is it? About the kidnapping?"

I barked again with a flick of my head, wishing I could shift back into my human form. Even if I had clothes to slip into, I didn't have the energy to transform. After running all over town, the threat in the note, and the shock of Judy's accusation, I had nothing left. Not even adrenaline coursed through my veins now as I stood in the safety of Sett's presence.

"Glowing? Screaming?" Hattie said, trying to understand me. I shook my head and barked again with a scratch at the ground. "Taken?"

I growled and scratched at the floor until Hattie finally landed on the right word. "Poof?" I needed them to understand my epiphany. Judy knew exactly what had happened to Senna because she'd done it to her, and the proof was in the pile of books. Anyone with a witch in their ancestry could learn to summon, and Judy was the queen of learning. Senna didn't just disappear—the state of her house, the missing items—all pointed to a summoning.

I jumped up, my forepaws landing on the desk as my claws clicked against the wood. With my snout pointed at the shelf above, I released another bark that simmered to a whimper.

"I'm requesting the book again, Judy," Sett said and, to my surprise, didn't wait for the librarian to retrieve it. Against library policy, he edged around the desk, stepping over the fallen books of witch history, magical lore, and more. Tall enough to reach the towering shelf, Sett merely stretched his arm above his head and plucked the grimoire from between two iron bookends of pirate ships.

"I don't think—" Judy started, but Sett held up a hand, and the mere look on his serious face shut down her argument.

I glanced at Judy, who held her face in her hands and slumped over the table in the center of the library. The collection of books matched Senna's house and the missing objects. Had the librarian really summoned Senna and then came back here only to lie about it? Why else did she have books with these specific objects? Was Senna close by? Tied up in the library's storage room or by the bushes in the back? My mind tumbled over theories, but none of them stuck.

Sett splayed the book open between us, and I scratched at the desk beside it. Despite his thick stony fingers, he both gently and quickly turned page after page until he reached the summoning section and I pawed at the book to stop there.

I scanned the words, refreshing my knowledge on the subject. *Each personal object is to be set in a circle. These are a few of her favorite things, and thus used to bring her forth by another's will with no consideration for the subject's own will. One moment here, the next gone.* A scribbled note in the margins answered my next question. *Objects of personal significance*

If Judy didn't like the fact that Senna had destroyed library property, maybe kidnapping her was punishment, and blaming me was the easiest course of action since Judy knew I was tracking the spell *and* at Fate's house the night he died. I pawed at the word to get Hattie talking again.

"Objects," the ghost said, confidently understanding me.

I barked at Judy, who did a little jump in her chair and dabbed at her watery nose with a crumpled napkin.

"Judy's objects?" Hattie guessed. "Books!"

I shook my head. If only I had the energy to shift, I could borrow Sett's coat and slip it over my naked body. But the weight of my own heavy limbs told me I still wasn't ready.

"Judy's books..." Hattie mumbled, trying to piece the puzzle together.

To Judy's dismay, I padded over to her chair and cocked my head. She lifted her lip in disgust and leaned away from me as she spoke. "She looks confused."

"Questions," Hattie said, understanding my gesture. I spun

and met the ghost's gaze, nodding for her to keep going. "Were there objects?" I hurried back to the books and gathered the magazine in my mouth, returning to drop it at Judy's feet. Next, I carefully carried *The Book of Prophecies* to her, keeping the pages open to the information on summoning. After repeating that with the two other odd books, I sat down in front of the librarian and growled.

The blood drained from Judy's face, leaving her freckles scattered over porcelain-white cheekbones. With a shaking hand, she adjusted her cat-frame glasses and cleared her throat. Beneath the table, she reached into her skirt's pocket. Ammonia filled the air as her hand remained tucked where I couldn't see, buried beneath layers of floral fabric.

Sett and Hattie gathered close, and I barked. *Where are the objects?* If we found the summoning circle—or diamond—we'd find the witch. We'd both save the kidnapped woman and likely locate the stolen spell.

"What does this mean?" Sett asked, pointing at the pile I'd collected. It looked like an offering to the all-powerful librarian.

A shiver stole through me. Did Judy really kill library patrons over a few pieces of stolen paper? The grimoire *was* considered the most sacred property regarding Bewitcher's Beach since I'd found it only weeks before. A sacred book damaged, stolen, and a passionate librarian with a penchant for horror stories...

"I don't know," Hattie said before she gasped. "Wait, I do know! This looks like the book series from the witch's house. And, and the thorned ivy!" Hattie set her sights on the culprit. "Judy must have summoned Senna."

I barked. *Bingo! Thank you, Hattie.*

Judy touched her heaving chest and tore her eyes from me, directing the answer to Sett. "I don't know what they're talking about."

The sudden and stifling odor of rotten fish filled my nose. The librarian lied. When she stood, shoving the chair back, I jumped to my feet and bared my teeth. Her eyes expanded to saucers of pale blue against a milky white as she backed away from me, hand still buried in her pocket. *Show us what you're hiding.*

"Miss Knovel, do you know something you're not telling us?" Sett asked.

"No!"

Another lie. The stench only grew stronger, causing me to gag as the oily, rancid smell settled on my tongue.

Growling rumbled within me, and my snout quivered with anger. *Tell us the truth!*

"I didn't kidnap her! I'm telling you, Noema is to blame. You're just too smitten with her to see it." Sett opened his mouth but Judy didn't let him get a word in. "Senna even told me she believes she saw Crow leaving Fate's house the night he died. And then lo and behold, Crow and Noema start going steady."

I couldn't suppress the growl that slipped out. Crow? *No.* Someone matching his figure had been walking the beach, but I didn't believe the lying Livid Librarian because she reeked of guilt. Crow was busy at Roller Shakes that night. And we were not going steady—it was one date!

Sett pinched his nose in frustration while Hattie folded her arms. The librarian's taut face washed to stoicism as she pursed her lips. The faux look of confidence didn't match the odor of fear and lies.

"You have to believe me," Judy said, still fiddling with something in her pocket. What was she hiding? Her eyes darkened as the scent of anger overwhelmed the mixture of ammonia and fish. Narrowing her gaze on Sett, she tugged at the object in her pocket. "Or else I'll have to—"

When her arm bent, all reason left me; instinct took over, and I dove for her. I dodged the chair between us and launched off my hind legs before she could pull a gun, a knife, a book with a really hard spine, or whatever weapon she'd concealed and now threatened the sheriff with. With my forepaws landing on her shoulders, we both went down.

"Noema!" Sett shouted.

Judy's hands splayed out behind her, but her elbows smacked against the geometric rug. Without thinking, I snapped at the object in her hand, ripping it from her grip. She shrieked, but I didn't stick around to let her take it back.

When I turned, I was eye level with Sett's crotch.

"Arrest that mutt!" Judy said. Instead, Sett side-stepped me and reached to help the librarian up while I spit the piece of paper out of my mouth. Soggy and torn, it fell to the sheriff's feet. Heat rippled through me as I realized I'd protected us from nothing more than a papercut.

Judy reached for it as she scrambled to her feet but, to my surprise, Sett was faster. He snagged the soggy scrap of paper and smoothed it out. After a moment of scanning the contents, his brow furrowed and he looked up at the librarian.

"Miss Knovel, enough is enough. You need to come down to the station."

CHAPTER 16
SUMMONING WARS: RETURN OF THE JUDY

Senna

- *Thorned ivy*
- *Romance novels*
- *Fashion*
- *Trophy*

Fate

- *Sketchbook*
- *Electrical wires*
- *Beer*
- *Trophy*

ONCE WE PIECED the torn paper together again, the list was complete. Complete proof of Judy's involvement with the summonings. Though she never needed to summon Fate. Just showing up at his house and shoving him into buzzing wires was enough to end him.

Sett carefully stored the list in the pocket of his blue coat and guided Judy out the door. Outside the station, he turned to us with a sigh.

Rain pelted the cobblestone and drowned the sound of his breath in white noise. His firm, deep voice cut through the elements as he fixed his eyes on me. "Thank you for your help. I'll be questioning Miss Knovel." A moment passed with only the storm's response. "I'd like you two to stay safe."

A groan and a huff escaped me. Of course he wanted that, but time was running out. If Judy didn't confess, Senna could be hurt, abandoned, trapped. My stomach twisted for the young witch I only wanted to protect.

"And right now, the safest place is with me," he continued. My ears perked and my tail lifted.

"Safe? You're here with the killer," Hattie, blunt as ever, said. A little grumble escaped me. *Don't convince him to send us away. I want to help and get answers about that spell!*

Sett swiped his palm over his chin and nodded. "While that's true, we don't have undeniable proof of Judy's crime yet and I"—his slate eyes slid to me—"worry. Both Senna and Fate have been targeted for working on the spell, and since Noema has been tracking it, I prefer to keep her safe rather than sorry." He cleared his throat and glanced in the distance before returning to meet my gaze. "Plus, Mayor Fitz wants to please everyone who voted for the holiday and continue, on the condition that we wrap up this investigation with enough time to set ghost traps. I need your help to get this solved sooner rather than later." My heart soared. Not only did Sett hint at reinstating the Ghost Pirate Moon invitation, but he was actually *asking* for my input. "I'll send Gemma to escort you back to the station after you get changed. Bring the kids with you. I'll wait to question Judy until you return."

I barked in agreement and Sett offered a curt nod before disappearing inside.

WHEN WE RETURNED TO MOCKBUSTER, I

relieved Bette of her babysitting, which had consisted of binging *Full House* episodes with the pups flopped on the couch in matching pirate pajamas.

In dry jeans and a warm hoodie, I gathered the kids with the promise of an "adventure at the police station." While Stevie grabbed Sir Crabby for the sleepover, Jovi brought a book he'd heard Sett read at the library during the sheriff's volunteer hours, and Halen snagged a science-fiction movie he knew the family friend would enjoy. Dio pounded down the stairs before everyone else, eager to visit the police officer he wanted to be like when he grew up. I trailed behind the pack of pups with a fresh can of Diet Pepsi in one hand and Squeaks in the other, ready to caffeinate and cuddle my way through a night of sniffing out a suspect.

As expected, the door chimed with our escort's arrival, but it wasn't the stern-faced cop who greeted us. Instead of a slick blonde ponytail, dark curls and even darker eyes met mine. Across the shop and over the heads of four pups, we shared a moment of hesitation. Crow offered a curt nod as a sly smile quirked his face. I returned the expression before I recalled how quickly he'd ditched our date. Not to mention the smell of death. My smile sagged.

"Hey, I wanted to apologize for skipping out on you the other night," he said as he waded through the crowd of kiddos. "Work called—"

I folded my arms. "Roller Shakes?"

"Uh." His eyes darted around, and he scrubbed at the back of his neck. "Not quite." Lavender. The scent of truth confirmed his response, and I knew I'd caught him in a sticky situation. "I was with Chanel."

I nodded, processing the odd explanation that smelled entirely truthful but also vague enough to conceal an upsetting answer. If he wanted to date us both at the same time, at least have the courtesy and courage to tell us. "With Chanel? Like seeing her?"

He laughed. "Seeing? I see her most days around town." I frowned. Understanding dawned as his dark eyes brightened. "OH! You mean *seeing* seeing? No, no. I was just helping her family. Her boyfriend really."

"You saw him?" The consistent aroma of lavender finally relaxed me. Crow didn't seem to be hiding anything, and my irritation shifted to curiosity. Nobody had ever met Chanel's wealthy and elderly boyfriend. Some even believed he wasn't real.

"*Seeing* saw? As in going steady? No. I mean, he was handsome for an older gentleman, but I just physically saw him when I helped out."

"I want to go on a seesaw!" Dio interrupted us.

Crow leaned closer, bringing that intoxicating scent of birch trees and rainstorms with him and not a hint of guilt or fear or anything that would suggest he was lying about helping Chanel's boyfriend. "Anyway, I was hoping the two of us could finish the movie...alone."

With the conversation now dubbed boring, Dio skipped away. He followed his brothers and sister out the door where they danced around in the rain. I should have worried about their soaked pjs and possible wet-dog smell, but Crow captured my attention.

Butterflies erupted in my stomach. "Alone?" I repeated. Though the idea was no different than the movie date we'd already shared, the gleam in his eyes and slight side-smile was suggestive.

Everything about Crow spelled trouble. He didn't share pieces of his past like Sett had warned. But did that make him dangerous? The darkness in his eyes hinted at the promise of one thing. The one thing that had me sworn off of dating and of falling for someone ever again. The one thing that took the love of my life away from me. As a werewolf, *I* was dangerous. And if it hadn't been for me, Christopher would still be alive. If he hadn't loved me, he'd never have become a wolf like me. And if he was never a wolf, he wouldn't have died from the silver in the antibiotics.

Crow stepped past me into the romance aisle, headed straight for the wall of new releases. Unlike Christopher, Crow and I shared a curious personality and a penchant for trouble. He glanced over his shoulder and flashed me a rakish grin before reaching for the *Alien* VHS tape.

"A second date?" I asked, getting ahead of myself as I followed him. *But you ditched our first date so suddenly...*

He turned, movie in hand extended toward me. "Exactly. But I've heard from You Know Who that you've sworn off dating, so I'm both surprised and flattered that you acknowledged it. Twice now."

Of course Mae had shared with him my promise to stay single. Though she barely knew the truth about Christopher and how if he hadn't been a werewolf for me, he would have survived, she still spread what she did know. Which was enough to signal to the entire town that I was permanently off the market. Still, it didn't deter Crow, and I couldn't help but appreciate his gutsy request. Even Sett never directly asked me on a date.

Finally, I shrugged and took the movie from him. "I'm in," I said with a matching half-smile. "But not tonight; I'm in the middle of a murder investigation."

His head tilted slightly, curls tumbling to one side. "A murder investigation with your kids in tow?"

Warmth filled me at the thought of Sett's suggestion. He was usually too protective, but I appreciated that he invited my whole crew to the station this time. "With my kids in tow," I repeated with a nod.

"Bummer." After shaking curls from his eyes, he offered me the same courtesy. He reached out and tucked an escaped lock of hair behind my ear. The action brought us closer with only a hair's breadth between our noses. I'd turned away from Sett's kiss, knowing I couldn't bear to ever hurt him the way I did Christopher.

But could I hurt Crow? Could I hurt someone who was a mirror of me? Could I throw caution to the stormy wind through the forest of birch trees and let myself soak in his scent? Even the sourness of death didn't stain him this time. I leaned into him, not wanting to miss the moment. When I didn't kiss Sett, he'd understood and stepped back, returning us to friendship with an underlying tension between our differences. Did I want Crow to step back?

I turned my chin, angling my mouth to his when his lips spread to a full grin and he leaned away. "But I guess I can wait."

My stomach dropped. The anchor returned.

He nodded to the windowed walls that lined the front of the shop where a shadow stood. A familiar smooth ponytail whipped in the storm's wind. Gemma squinted through the glass at us, waiting with her thumbs tucked into her belt.

Once our eyes met, she unhooked her hand and waved for me to come outside.

"Right," I said, clearing my throat and washing away the embarrassment and butterflies and tension of the moment.

"I didn't want an audience," he said. "Alone, remember? Like a real date."

For once, that sounded good. Just the two of us without Squeaks' chirping input and Sir Crabby's interruptions. A night with a new friend, a new movie, and a date without having to share our tub of popcorn with the pups. Of course, Sett never minded sharing and always brought extra homemade snacks. But Sett wasn't the man standing in front of me suggesting a date.

As we walked side-by-side to the exit, our hands bumped and I felt like a twenty-year-old again...until the earthy scent of decay prickled my nose. Did he always smell of death and I'd willfully ignored it at times? Sudden memory of Sett's warning —Crow's supposed secrets—sent a shiver down my spine.

We exited and parted ways as Gemma implored me to hurry. The cop popped open a wide umbrella and demanded I get beneath it. The pups huddled close too, except for Stevie who let Sir Crabby enjoy the raindrops washing over him.

The six of us hurried through the storm and to the station. While the pups gathered around the small TV on a table beside Sett's desk to watch *Nick at Nite,* a slew of Nickelodeon shows, I followed Gemma to the back room. The small station only had a front lobby with the sheriff's desk, a small kitchen area, a storage closet, and a restroom, while the back half housed a single jail cell and a near-empty room with only a table and three chairs. It wasn't the homiest and yet my kids settled right in as if visiting a family member.

Despite my fear for the young witch and disappointment over the missing spell, my heart was full. Crow flattered me, the pups enjoyed a fun sleepover at the station, and Sett trusted me enough to invite me into this murder investigation. If I met the family I couldn't remember soon—if the pirate Annette was truly my ancestor—my heart might burst.

When Gemma pointed to the closed door, I peered through the thin, rectangular window to see Sett sitting opposite the librarian.

"Is this an interrogation room?" I asked, wondering if the back storage closet had been transformed since I'd last visited the station.

Gemma frowned. "Sett doesn't like it when we call it that but essentially that's what I cleared it out for, yes. He calls it the questioning quarters. Something of which he requested your help on."

One glance at the pile of pups lounging on the sheriff's desk chair or laying belly-down on the floor told me they were both safe and content.

Turning back to Gemma, I said, "And you're okay with me helping?" I pointed to my collarbone and then to the interrogation *closet*.

With a blink and an eye roll, she said, "I wasn't at first, but I've recently realized it's not a big deal."

Lavender. Calm, floral, fresh, and light enough to prove Gemma truly didn't care about my involvement anymore. Though I was curious what had changed her mind, I didn't stick around to ask. Of course, if it were Sett who convinced her of my skill and desire to help—if it'd locate the protection spell faster—I wanted to thank him. After all, we were true *friends*.

Gemma twisted the knob with her back still against the door and opened it, allowing me to step through. It was no surprise when Judy's frown deepened at the sight of me. Either she worried I'd sniff out her lies and catch her once and for all, or she held firm to that rivalry grudge. I still didn't understand how movies and books needed to be at odds rather than coexist for a variety of entertainment options.

Sett stood and pulled the other chair out for me before leaning on the table with his stony knuckles crackling.

"Do you care to explain what *she* is doing here?" Judy asked, hatred lacing her voice.

Sett opened his mouth, but Gemma beat him to the punch. From the open doorway, she sighed and said, "Because this station is too podunk to afford a polygraph machine. Don't worry, Noema won't be around long." To Sett, she mimicked the shape of a phone at her ear with her thumb and pinky finger protruding. "I'll be waiting for the phone call with the test results."

With a slam of the door, she announced her exit, and her ponytail vanished from the little window.

If life was like a movie, we'd play "good cop, bad cop" and manipulate the answer out of the suspect while a dim light bulb blinked between us. Instead, Sett ran through a slew of general questions, much like when a culprit was first tested on a polygraph machine. Finally, he dove deeper, asking Judy of her whereabouts the night Fate died, how well she knew him, and what she was researching with the collection of books she'd gathered.

She was at the library. Lavender scent? *Check.*

My heart skipped. "Wait." Their eyes slid to me, expectant. "When you told me you arrived at the library late that day, you..." I glanced at Sett. "You smelled guilty."

With a scoff, Judy flicked a flyaway strand of red hair from her eyelashes and then pinned me with her gaze. "That's because I blamed myself for the damage to those precious books. I take it personally to preserve each and every single page in that library."

"What about Senna's phone number? You told me you didn't have it but then you gave it to Mae."

She bubbled a laugh. "Because Mae asked nicely. You growl and bark and sell...movies." Though she spoke as if the word was poison on her tongue, the fresh aroma of a meadow on a spring day emanated from Judy like warm rays of sunshine. Judy was telling the truth, so I offered Sett a curt nod. He continued. The questions revealed Fate had studied at the library occasionally and Judy had spoken with him when she wanted to learn more about witch magic.

Truth? *My nose knows.* Judy was as calm as *Star Trek*'s Data when the android relayed technical information. She explained her research as interest in the capabilities of a witch. The calming scent that'd confirmed her answers before now faded and regret's smell of burnt toast filled the room.

I glanced at Sett with a faint arch to my eyebrow. *Something's off.*

Without so much as a nod, I knew he understood. Sett turned his attention to the suspect and repeated a similar question. "Why exactly did you want to learn more about witch magic?"

Judy sucked in a sharp breath and wrinkled her nose. "Because I am a student of life and just wanted to learn. I am a librarian!"

Truth. Lie. Truth.

The rapid shift of Judy's emotions left me sneezing. As fast as the stench of ammonia had arisen sandwiched between whiffs of lavender, it vanished and was replaced by a new smell. *Confidence.* The warm, amber scent of sandalwood overwhelmed everything else. Judy shifted to the edge of her chair, folded her arms on the table, and leaned closer to us. "If you want to find the real suspect, I suggest checking the list of people who requested *The Book of Prophecies.*"

I knew that list like the back of my paw, and the only person left on it that wasn't law enforcement, the woman in front of us, dead, summoned, or me was...*Crow*. My stomach felt as deep as the ocean as my heart fell and fell and fell. *Crow doesn't have a motive, and he barely knew Fate and Senna.*

Sett tucked his wings tightly to his body and took a seat. "Why do you say that?"

"Because, they're the only ones who'd know how to summon, and I didn't do it." She grimaced as if she'd tasted a sour fruit. "And if you must know, yes, I learned how to summon. It is what the lists were for. Senna and I were preparing a stunt—" A gasp escaped me as she teetered on a confession. "Nothing dangerous."

Before she could explain more, the door swung open and Gemma marched inside. She bumped my chair as she walked past, though there was plenty of room to get around the table. Her gaze narrowed on Judy, who continued, unfettered by the cop's glare. "As I was saying, they were working for some teacher's trophy in witch school or whatever, and when I found out about that, I had the brilliant idea to..."

Her voice faded from my ears as my attention split. With Gemma draped over Sett's shoulder, she whispered into his ear. I tilted my ear to catch her faint words. "The lab called. It is confirmed; Judy's fingerprints were all over the wires and Fate's house."

"Are you listening to me?" Judy snapped her fingers at us, reaching across the table. My ears flicked forward, perked by the sudden loud voice from the soft-spoken librarian. She shook her head and adjusted her new star-framed glasses. Her demand didn't deter Gemma, who still spoke in hushed tones, but I couldn't concentrate on both at once, and Judy held my gaze with the intensity of her insistent stare. A palpable stench filled the room, thick and heavy like a blanket of rotten fish flesh. I coughed and raised my hand to my nose to block the odor of lies.

Judy continued. "I teamed up with the witch to use the spells in *The Book of Prophecies* to show people how powerful and important books can be. I was going to summon both of them into the library for a show. And then poor Fate...well, you know the rest. Fate didn't know about the stunt, and I thought it would be a nice *surprise* to knock some sense into that boy after he'd caused a ruckus at the library. I knew it looked bad that I had this planned and then he was killed, so I kept it to myself. Not even Senna knew I was going to rope him into it."

Poor Senna was caught in the middle of multiple schemes —mine included. I never should have asked her to recreate the spell.

"But I wasn't the only one who didn't like that troublemaker!" Judy interrupted my thoughts. "Crow complained about Fate's behavior at Roller Shakes too. A bit suspicious, if I do say so myself."

I sucked in a breath. *Crow?* The fishy smell subsided, but my stomach soured as if I'd just taken a bite right out of the lie. But it was the truth that twisted my gut. Crow was the only name left on the list, and according to my nose, Judy was calm, cool, and collected. Had he lied about why he requested the grimoire? He'd claimed the recipes interested him, but maybe it was the skill of summoning he truly wanted.

Gemma coughed and then quickly smoothed her hand over her slicked hair. Her sharp eyes flicked to the suspect. "Are you confessing that the warlock worked with you to summon the victims?"

"Which warlock?" Judy asked, brow knitting. "Fate is dead..."

The cop grimaced and leaned on the table with her knuckles. "Crow, the warlock at the roller rink."

"Crow said he's human." I piped up.

Gemma shook her head, ponytail twitching as she waved her hand. "I can't keep you supernaturals straight." She stood to her full height, and her gaze fell to me. "I think we've had enough of amateur hour anyway."

Sett's chair creaked as he stood and folded his arms. "We'll take a break."

While Gemma tugged Judy out of her seat and roughly poked her toward the door and then the jail cell across the hall, Sett guided me to the counter in the front room. He flipped over two mugs on a drying rack by the little sink and plucked a pot of cold coffee from the machine. Before I could protest, he finished pouring one cup and yanked the mini fridge's door open, producing a bottle of Diet Pepsi.

"It appears we've caught the killer," he said. The fizzy soda filled the plain white mug, and he lifted the other chipped coffee mug to his lips for a sip. I picked up the soda but didn't drink, instead running my finger along the rim, which also had a chip in it. "But Senna is still missing, and I worry she's trapped in a summoning diamond. I'll send Gemma to search Miss Knovel's home and see if we can track where Senna might be." He looked from his coffee to meet my gaze.

"I can help look for her. It's not interfering with the investigation if I say I'm still tracking the spell, right?" I glanced at Gemma, who emerged from the back of the station.

Sett leaned close enough to whisper. "Be careful."

It was a hint that he trusted me. Again. My heart was definitely going to burst. As he pulled back and lifted the mug for another sip, his eyes sparkled with knowing.

"I smelled a lie in the interrogation—the questioning room," I said, swallowing the lump in my throat. As much as I didn't want the killer to be my new *friend*, and the first man gutsy enough to actually ask me on a date since I'd moved here, I couldn't deny the clues. "Judy might be hiding something else, but she was telling the truth about Crow possibly being at Fate's house. I don't want to believe he's a suspect, but I saw someone—"

Sett held up his palm to stop me and turned his head because Gemma shouted for him, asking where a particular piece of paperwork had been moved to. He apologized and, with his free hand, he gently cupped my arm before nodding to the pile of pups. "I've got to process this paperwork and then we can talk again. They're safe here. You remember what I said."

Be careful.

CHAPTER 17
SENNA JAMES AND THE DIAMOND OF DOOM

SENNA'S SAFETY CAME FIRST. As I stepped out of the station and felt the uneven cobblestone beneath my feet, fierce wind whipped a sheet of rain beneath the overhang, soaking my shoes and pants. The storm raged, dumping in a curtain of heavy drops and threatening to flood the town square.

Crow was my first stop to finding Senna and the spell, and if that meant I had to swallow my hope and question the man I nearly kissed, I would. I would rip the missing pages right out of his hands. But I would do it with the weight of disappointment and a dash of embarrassment. I barely knew him. How could I let myself agree to a date with a stranger? A *suspect*. A man who smelled of death and decay. *But also birch trees, and forests, and freedom.*

Outside of Roller Shakes, swing shift employees darted to their cars or huddled under umbrellas as they walked home. I emerged from the shadows and hurried inside to find an open booth. Even at the late hour, the diner still buzzed with business. I unzipped my raincoat and slipped onto the vinyl seat on one side of an empty booth.

Cordelia, the night shift server, rolled over to me on bright purple skates with a fanged, beaming smile on her face. Our conversation was brief but fueled my determination. Like me, the young mother had been looking forward to the holiday celebration. If only we had the protection spell...

I indulged in a slice of pumpkin pie and waited for Crow to emerge from the little office in the back of the roller rink. Once he came out, I'd wave him down, invite him to sit, and sniff out the answers to a few casual questions.

The office door finally opened, and Crow stepped out. When I waved, he flashed me a tight smile but didn't come over. Instead, he covered the distance from the office to the exit in only a few long strides, completely bypassing the diner section altogether. He didn't so much as return my wave.

The downward curve of his lips betrayed his usual devil-may-care attitude, and the slight lift of his shoulders showed tension. He buried his hands in his pockets and shouldered his way out the door.

I dug a few dollars from my pockets and dropped them on the table before stalking after him. The rain had lifted, drizzling now in a gentle and soothing mist. I opened my mouth to call after him but clamped it shut. In the parking lot, Crow skipped his car and headed straight into the wooded area behind Roller Shakes. His tall frame melted into the low-hanging fog that coated the edge of the thick tree line.

"Where the heck is he going?" I muttered. I flipped my coat's hood over my head and stepped into the parking lot's puddles. Following him alone was risky, but I didn't have time to grab Hattie or Sett to accompany me before Crow vanished into the maze of trees.

With every step, puddle water soaked through the soft spot of my sneakers, and my socks squished. I kept a steady distance behind Crow's figure as he moved through the foggy woods.

Remaining rainwater relentlessly dripped from the tips of wide leaves, concealing the sound of my steps. Soft earth and the bright moss that covered the forest floor helped cover my clumsy heavy walk too.

The spread of thick bigleaf maples provided plenty of hiding spaces in case he turned. The urge to run ahead and question him rose, but I tamped it down. *Patience. Patience.*

But the more I said it and the further we delved into the middle of the shadowed forest, the more my nerves buzzed. Ammonia's odor trailed me. As I dared closer to Crow, the burning ick of urine mingled with his emotions. Deep, heavy sadness filled the air with the smell of rain and wet earth, doubling that of the aftermath of the storm's scent. The intensity of it told me this wasn't from the rain but straight from a broken heart, or grief, or pure depression.

In one whiff, I went from being suspicious of Crow to wanting to run ahead and throw my arms around him in an all-encompassing bear hug. Maybe it wasn't logical, but the smell of emotions often triggered similar emotions within me. All thoughts of comfort and hugs washed away when we came to a clearing between the trees.

Crow stepped into the open space of moss and dirt. And Senna.

A knot twisted my gut as everything I'd suspected came to light. "No." The word came out in a breath of hot air that mixed into the dense fog. *Crow, how could you? Why?* The strange sadness emanating from him didn't match the scene that unfolded before me.

On the ground lay a limp witch. Even lifeless, Senna looked like a woman on the cover of a magazine, dressed in designer fashion and with her hair in a braided crown that framed her forehead. Dug-out moss surrounded her in a diamond, and at each point were the items from the list found in Judy's pocket. A clip of thorned ivy, a destroyed copy of a romance novel titled *Cowboy's Crush*, a folded cashmere sweater, and a small trophy of a woman playing tennis.

Crow stood at the edge and stretched his arm out as if offering his hand to dance with a woman. But the only woman in front of him was dead. The realization sparked a scream that I stifled with a bite of my lips. My fanged canines dug a little too deeply into my skin and a soft yelp escaped me, but Crow either didn't notice or didn't care. He remained focused, eyes fixed on the space above Senna's body where there was nothing but a strange section of parted fog.

All at once, the fog filled in and Crow's hand fell limp at his side. He tilted his head to the woman at his feet, and my gaze followed, landing on Senna's chest as it rose with erratic but distinct breaths.

"She's alive," I whispered. Before I even finished breathing the words, Crow was gone. Had he heard me and ran? The break of a branch pulled my attention from the witch and to the sound of footsteps running fast and heavy through the forest. Crow ran and ran from his crime, leaving Senna summoned and barely hanging onto life. Sickness roiled in my belly. I'd trusted Crow, and I'd shirked Sett and Gemma's warnings about him. But I didn't have time to dwell on my mistake.

I shoved through branches and into the opening, kicking the stupid trophy from the diamond's point to break the summoning trap from the outside. I fell to her side. Only then did I notice the blood crusted on the back of her head.

"You were hit," I said to nobody. *Nobody.* I was the only one here. It was up to me to get Senna to safety, and fast. I shouldn't move her, but I couldn't leave her alone. What if Crow came back to finish the job?

It was time to get help, even if that meant I had to leave her. Planning to race through the trees as fast as four legs could carry me, I stood and shifted. My clothes fell to the ground as I dropped to all fours. Twice as fast now, I loped through the woods. Weaving between gnarled tree trunks, I finally burst through the persistent fog and within sight of buildings.

Thankfully, the clinic was on this side of town, and Dr. Pitt, the werebulldog clinician, hadn't left yet. I howled outside the door until he swung it open. The doctor, huge and hulking, followed suit. He shifted into his canine form to cover ground quicker with the handle of a first-aid kit in his snout.

Unlike me, Dr. Pitt had come prepared with a secondary outfit packed into his kit. After examining Senna, he ducked into the cover of nearby trees to shift and change. While he carried the patient back to the clinic, I padded alongside him, breaking off the path only to howl outside the station and alert Sett.

The sheriff opened the door just as Dr. Pitt disappeared with Senna inside the clinic next door.

She's alive. I barked. *And I know who did it.*

CHAPTER 18
MAN IN BLACK

THE NEXT MORNING, the clouds parted and the sun shone through. Likely, Sett had arrested Crow. Or had at least taken him in for interrogation—*questioning*. I wouldn't know, since Gemma insisted amateurs take their kids and go home.

So I'd gone home, and I didn't hate the fact that I finally got a bit of sleep. Too much, in fact. I'd slept through the morning while the pups watched a slew of Saturday Morning cartoons. They were careful not to wake me so they didn't miss a single episode between *Power Rangers* and *Darkwing Duck*.

While the pups played tag at the park with Bette, I headed to the clinic to check on the victim. After I'd shared what I witnessed with Sett, he'd presented the possibility of Crow and Judy working together. Evidence pointed to her, and what I'd witnessed pointed to him. "If there is more than one culprit, more than one killer, that's all the more reason to keep the holiday canceled," he'd said. He wasn't wrong, but I hated to hear the truth. Smelling it? Delightful. Hearing it? Not so much.

I shoved the thought away and marched into the clinic, hoping to find Senna alive and well.

Relief flooded me as I stepped inside and saw her in bed at the back. The small clinic only had one examination room to the right, a single front desk, and three beds behind that with curtains framing each one for privacy. Senna was the only patient today, and a cheerful one, at that. The witch flipped through *Sorcery and Style* magazine with one hand and sipped from a juice box with the other. A clean white bandage was wrapped around her head like a crown of survival.

Before I could march across the clinic and ask her what she remembered, the door opened behind me. Sett ducked through the doorway, keeping his wings tucked close to his body in the tight space.

I met his gaze. "Did you find Crow?"

His wings flickered as he answered with a slight shake of his head. "He's gone."

"Gone?" *He must have seen me.* He could have been anywhere by now, far away from Bewitcher's Beach. "You were right about him. He had a secret."

"But no motive." Sett took the words right out of my mouth. "Judy has already admitted to hating people who damage books. In fact, I've been called to the library multiple times to break up a fight between her and a patron who nicked a book's spine or accidentally dropped a book. She's not above slapping a reader. That's part of why I volunteer there, to keep an eye on her temper. And for the kids, of course."

"But I saw Crow at Senna's summoning diamond," I said. "He knew exactly where she was and he wasn't there to help her. He didn't even try to see if she was okay."

"And maybe he was an accomplice, like I said last night. That's why I'm here to get a more complete picture from the victim herself." With a slight tilt of his head, he invited me to come with him. Sett pushed through the half-door between the front counter and the wall. It swung back-and-forth in his wake as he strode to the back of the clinic.

Senna set down her juice box and greeted us. Showers of gratitude poured from her. "I would be dead if it wasn't for you." She reached for my hand and squeezed it. "It was really punk rock of you to save my life like that."

I smirked. Heavy music like punk rock was one of mine and Christopher's favorite things. Mention of it made me realize Senna and I were more alike than her fashion and my drab hoodies had me believing.

The conversation quickly darkened. Sett questioned what she'd witnessed, and Senna's eyes shifted between us. "I suppose it is possible Judy was the one who summoned me. She knew how. We'd even practiced it together so that she could pull off a little show for the library. We're friends, though, so if she hit me..." She carefully cupped her palm around the bandages at the back of her head and winced. "It would be because the magic had gotten to her head. I've heard non-witches who dabble can lose track of reality pretty easily."

I nodded, recalling the same information I'd read straight from *The Book of Prophecies* itself. "And what about Crow? I overheard you asking Judy about him."

Senna frowned. "It's embarrassing. I heard someone call him a warlock. I hoped it was true and that he could help with my project after Fate...died. Anyway, Crow's not a warlock. It was just a stupid rumor or something."

"Can I ask about Shadowvale?" I dared, encouraged by her mention of the school project. "Who is your coach, and what trophy were you and Fate competing for?"

She blinked rapidly, and the delicious scent of excitement filled the air. Banana cream pie's sweet aroma wafted from her. "Coach is just what we call the head witch. She—or he, I've never met them. They leave us challenges to practice, and whoever achieves them gets better marks in classes." She reached for the juice box, taking another sip before continuing. "We lived on campus at Shadowvale University. It's small; most people don't know about it, and most of our teachers are actually humans who have learned the history of people with magic. But the Coach runs it, and occasionally, we will practice some spells. When Fate and I heard a rumor that *The Book of Prophecies* was found, we had to come to town to see it. This could change the course of magic as our generation has known it. But nobody else believes it's the real one. I didn't know he was planning to plagiarize it until he pressured me to keep quiet about it."

The real one? Could the book be a fake? I shook my head and tried to think positively. The spells definitely worked, as proven by the successful summonings. And maybe Senna had the answers I was looking for. Maybe she knew more about the book's history and who had written it—whose hands wrapped a scarf around me and whose rose-scented perfume I smelled from the memories the pages sparked.

Sett cleared his throat. "Well, it seems this conversation is no longer telling of the investigation, so I'll leave you two to it. I've got an accomplice to investigate." A shudder rippled through me at the reference to Crow's crime. I tried to forget about it—and him.

After saying goodbye, Sett ducked out the door, and I turned to Senna. My pulse, fast and heavy, thudded in my ears as the hope for answers came within my grasp. Maybe if I couldn't meet Annette from the Drunken Oyster, someone at Senna's college would recognize me. If I was really the canine mentioned in the chosen prophecy...

"Do you know who wrote *The Book of Prophecies?*" The words came out in a squeak as my throat tightened. Was I getting ahead of myself? Too excited for a slim chance at finding my family? If the memories from the grimoire's smells were just hopeful delusions or daydreams, the whole theory that I was related to the creators could be a bust.

Senna's mouth spread into a brilliant smile. "Know them? Lulu is a legend."

Lulu? The memories flashed quickly one after another, and I tried to picture a face with that name on my tongue. It felt familiar and warm but I couldn't place it.

"A 'legend'? As in not real?"

She laughed. "You sound like humans before those of us with magic and powers came out of hiding! Or at least what I've heard from history books about those times. Lulu was a real witch, or is, but she was very private. We only know that she either wrote or contributed to *The Book of Prophecies* because that's what Coach tells us."

"Is there no way to contact her?"

Senna shook her head.

"What about the prophecy about the chosen witches with the pirate and the...person who can smell intentions? Do you know much about that?"

"I know enough to wish I was chosen," she said as she tugged at her hospital gown to reveal the bat wing mark. She tilted her head toward it and sighed. "Some of us at Shadowvale dared each other to get tattoos and pretend. A chosen witch can see the future, and the legend says that the mark that appears on her predicts the next chosen witch. So I'm pretending I'll have a shapeshifter child someday." A little grin danced on her lips until she wiped it away and the smell of embarrassment rose. "That was dumb, though, because now Ted and I aren't even dating anymore." She muttered it more to herself than to me and then glanced at me before rolling her eyes. "He's a shapeshifter."

The next chosen. Had someone been marked with a werewolf sign? Was it my mother? Still, the name Lulu felt familiar. Like someone I'd read about in a book or seen on TV, but not as close as a family member. Certainly not a mother or the person in my memories. It was wishful thinking at best because the biggest hole in my theory was my lack of witchiness. If I had a witch in my ancestry, I'd likely have hints of magic show through. Like Judy, who must have had traces of witch in her bloodline since she was capable of summoning.

Or Crow...who could have been her accomplice.

All at once, the hope I'd felt when the sun came out this morning vanished, and a weighted sadness settled over my muscles. One strong enough to sap me of energy and make it impossible to shift into my wolf form no matter how much I longed to run on the beach and howl away my troubles for a few minutes.

When Dr. Pitt came to the other side of Senna's bed with a stethoscope and a pain pill in a little cup, I thanked them both and slipped out.

Already, gray clouds blocked out the sun to match my mood, and the park was empty. I caught sight of a wolf's tail disappearing inside Everland Theater, likely following after Bette. She'd put them to work dusting chairs with their tails before they played on their Game Boys.

Allowing my mind to wander helped soothe the sting of last night's discovery. But only a little. A run on all fours with salt-water in my fur would help a lot. Unfortunately, the weight of realization still sapped my energy. I merely dragged myself into Mockbuster and dropped onto the stool behind the counter. According to the hours printed on the sign that hung by the door, the shop should be open right now.

There was nothing I could do now except wait for Sett to find Crow with the spell and hope Madam Rowena showed up before the new moon.

I sighed and stood again, ready to continue a regular workday for the sake of movie-loving renters. After all, I didn't want the last couple of days of the business's boom to end because of inconsistent hours. Finding my family, celebrating Bewitcher's Beach's pirate ancestors, and even the murder investigation would have to wait.

I yanked the sign's dangling chain, and the bright colors gently lifted my spirits. If nothing else, I could count on my shop to comfort me. The faint, lingering smell of popcorn, the wall of delicious candy and sodas, and rows and rows of my favorite thing in the entire world—movies. And once I finished those, maybe I'd finally—finally—sit down to work on my screenplay.

With a slight skip in my step, I decided I'd let go of the disappointment. Just for today, I'd forget it all and indulge in a bag or two of popcorn while I finished inventory. The task was tedious, but it gave me the delight of going through all the movies I'd forgotten. The old movies. The movies I'd watched with Christopher and the kids and Sett.

After preparing a bowl of butter-dripping popcorn upstairs, I returned to the shop. I settled on the floor of the action aisle to continue where I left off. Between each inventory scan, I munched on the salty snack and wiped the excess butter off on a napkin tucked under the bowl. Dusk fell as I finally finished the task. Relief over a project well done didn't come, and I paced the aisles, double-checking the placements of the movies. With so much on my mind, I couldn't keep still.

Gentle rain sprinkled the windowed walls, stopping and starting in moody fits.

The heaviness slowly crept back in as I passed the spot where Crow had asked me on a date. The weight pulled harder at my heart and shoulders as I compared my life to some of my favorite films. Though I loved science fiction exploration, action blasts, and the laughter from comedies, nothing quite lived up to stories about families.

I found myself drifting to the family section, where my favorite movies were shelved. I reached for *The Princess Bride*, but the place was empty. The space was even missing the VHS dummy copy, which was unusual considering the dummy copies were empty cases with no tape inside. The cover copy was intended only to fill the shelf. It showed customers the original cover of the movie while the actual VHS tapes were stored in basic black cases wrapped with the yellow and blue colors of my shop. It must have gone missing after I finished that aisle of inventory. Hopefully, I wouldn't have to start over.

"Weird," I muttered as I headed for the register to check the records. Another hole on the shelf caught the corner of my eye, and I stopped mid-step. I crouched and checked behind the neighboring VHS tapes. *The Lion King* was missing too, along with its original dummy case.

Maybe the kids had collected all of my favorites for a surprise movie night with mommy. But I'd never listed these as my favorites before, at least not until I'd tried to come up with a top three.

Hattie phased through the back wall, silently announcing her entrance with the dancing reflections of her glittery dress. The golden sparkles brightened the floor and walls as she surged forward and stopped behind me. The icy chill of her spirit cooled me, bringing a temporary sense of calm.

"I heard Senna has recovered quickly. Did she have amnesia or anything?" she asked.

"Thankfully, none, just some pain, I imagine. We got to her before the bleeding was too bad."

Hattie's voice shifted from curious to curiouser. "What are you doing down there? Didn't you just organize that? I'm not saying Judy has a right to judge your messiness, but Noema..."

I halted the hunt for the movie and squinted up at her. "*The Princess Bride* and *Lion King* are missing their dummy copies."

"And *The Breakfast Club*," Hattie said. She pointed at another hole on the shelf one aisle over in the comedy section.

I stood and hurried to the computer, where Squeaks lay curled on top of the warm screen. Apparently, he'd given up sneering at Sir Crabby for the evening. As I circled to the other side of the desk, I reached to give pets to my fuzzy little companion.

The moment my hand landed between his ears and on the soft fur of his head, my stomach flipped upside down. Hattie's voice shouted from miles away, as if she screamed at me from the other side of a long train tunnel. The words were indistinguishable, and my head spun until everything went black and my stomach flipped upside down again.

A sudden chilly wind swept over my back, and I knew I was no longer inside Mockbuster.

Before I opened my eyelids, I felt something soft under my hand. But this time, it was damp. Droplets of icy water pattered the side of my cheek and the back of my neck.

"Squeaks?" I muttered. All energy had been sapped from me as if I'd just shifted from human to wolf and back again a dozen times in a row. Waves of dizziness washed over me as I peeled my eyes open.

Instead of the mouse's fuzzy head, my hand cupped a mound of moss. My vision adjusted to an object a foot away. A single can of Diet Pepsi sat nestled into a divot of mud. Irregular pulse thumped in my ears, and every muscle in my body tightened. I peeled my cheek off the forest floor, craning my neck with the little strength I had to see the items surrounding me.

A stack of VHS tapes.

A soccer ball.

And a spiral-bound notebook.

I'd been summoned—no, worse. *Trapped.* Pressure pounded in my skull as a shadow stood over me. Despite the pain radiating through my temples, I twisted my head to look up.

The dim glow of the moon broke through the forest's thick branches in scattered places. Above me, all light was blocked by a familiar frame. In the shadows, I could make out the spiral shape of curls and a hard jawline. My eyes adjusted to the darkness, and I saw my kidnapper—the killer.

As usual, Crow only smirked.

CHAPTER 19
BACK TO HIS FUTURE

ADRENALINE RIPPLED THROUGH ME, boosting me with enough energy to shift into my wolf form and defend myself. I resisted the urge to grow claws and fangs and fur and did my best to stay level-headed. As a wolf, I could growl and snap my jaws, but I couldn't talk a murderer down from the act of killing.

Crow turned his back to me and sighed. How could he summon me here? I truly hadn't known him at all.

I tensed and composed myself, pulling my feet beneath me to stand and face him. If he was going to hurt me for a reason I still could not place, I wanted him to look me in the eye first. Besides, I'd had enough of running into people's rear ends for one holiday season.

Pressure pounded in my forehead and the back of my skull as I dragged myself to sitting. I gently rubbed my head, but the pain didn't increase and no blood came back on my hand. I wasn't hit like Senna.

"Why?" I asked, my voice cracking. "I smelled death on you, but I don't understand why you killed Fate or tried to kill Senna." Was he the one who removed the protection over

Bewitcher's Beach? The one who stopped those with magic from recreating it? I focused on him again, but he was still faced away, hand pinching his head. The cover of crossed branches and thick trees blocked most of the misty rain, but a stygian fog clung just above the ground, slowly soaking my curls and clothes. "Why me? I'm not a witch or a warlock."

"What?" He turned. His thick brows pulled to the center with a crease in between, and his dark eyes sharpened as he narrowed his gaze on me.

I tried to blink the foggy vision from my eyes, but the summoning left the world tilting my vision, and my head was slow to catch up.

"Are you one of those rogue hunters who wants to kill supernatural people?" I asked. Crow ran his fingers through his hair and pulled his other hand from his pocket. Protective instinct had me raising my palm to stop him. "Wait! I just want to understand! You don't have to kill me; I can't recreate the spell..." A wave of dizziness crashed over me, leaving me to blink away black spots. As much as I wanted to be related to the people who wrote the grimoire, as much as I wanted to be *that* werewolf mentioned in the prophecy, the memories were not facts or proof of anything.

"Noema, I'm not—" He stepped forward.

I held my quivering hand out as if it could stop him from getting any closer. "I know the smell of death; you always carry it with you." He crouched only a few steps in front of me. Too close for comfort. "Are you a hunter?" I repeated.

"Noema."

"Or a serial killer?"

His jaw tensed, and all at once, he burst, his fingers curling in frustration. "I'm a reaper!" His hands shot out toward me. Despite my instinct to recoil, he didn't attack. He didn't even reach me.

"A reaper," I echoed. "A grim reaper..." My muddled mind tried to piece together the puzzle of Crow's life—or rather, how he dealt with those who'd lost theirs. Was this the truth? I tried to smell for lavender, but only the ammonia of fear stung my nose. I couldn't confirm his claim, and he fell silent, sighing gently with his head dropped to his hands as he stood again.

The world spun. After a moment, I squinted at the VHS tapes. As expected, *The Princess Bride*, *The Lion King*, and *The Breakfast Club* were stacked one on top of the other in their dummy cases with the original movie cover.

Had Crow taken them when he'd visited me yesterday? Bette never would have allowed anyone to rent a tape in its dummy case. Of course, I'd never told him the names of my favorite films. There were simply too many...

Blood left my face, draining all at once as shock threatened to pick up the world around me and take me for another carousel ride without my permission. There was only one person I'd told about my favorite movies. The person who insisted. The person I'd suspected but always wrote off as Sett's friend and as one who found and brought killers to justice—not someone who became one. The person talented at acting, or rather, talented at *everything*. Everything from hiding her crimes behind her investigative work to summoning.

"Gemma," I breathed. I'd assumed my initial suspicion was fueled by jealousy and had shoved the signs away.

My legs wobbled but adrenaline kept me upright as I straightened, and my gaze fell to the other objects on the forest floor. The same diamond shape surrounded Crow with an item at each point. He paced inside the summoning trap between a bottle of whiskey, boxing gloves, a copy of *Alien* also in its dummy case, and car keys.

He turned to me with a grim smile. His expression hadn't changed, but the trick of shadows and fear had me believing I'd seen an arrogant countenance. I'd mistaken his taut look for a smirk.

With a nod he said, "Yes, Gemma was here earlier." Ammonia blocked his usual birchwood smell and the hint of death buried beneath the stench of fear. The death smell that came with being a reaper; I knew that now. "She left right after she summoned you to..." His Adam's apple bobbed with a hard swallow, and finally, his gaze met mine. Dark eyes fixed on me with a weight tugging at the corners. "To get a weapon, because you're dangerous." He frowned and tore his gaze away from me for a moment, his jaw flexing and fingers curling into fists. His breath caught, and he faced me again. "Those were her words, not mine. I suspect she's getting silver bullets."

My ears pulled back, dragging some of the curls toward the back of my skull as they pressed against my head. What did Gemma want with me? I shoved the thought away, having just barely digested Crow's confession. I thought Crow was a human, perhaps with a witch or warlock ancestor, but not a reaper. Reapers were rare, chosen only by The Unnamed Witch and destined to guide people's souls to the afterlife rather than get stuck wandering the world in confusion. The smell of death made sense. When he'd suddenly leave a situation like during our date... *he was being drawn away by his calling.* "Is that why you left during our movie night? To reap someone's soul?" I finally gathered enough strength in my legs to stand.

Crow raked his hands through his thick curls and sucked in a breath. "Yes. Chanel's boyfriend needed me. Thankfully, he'd lived a very long life and passed away in his sleep at ninety-nine."

"It was you that night on the shore. I—I thought I saw you walking near Fate's house, but I assumed it was someone else because it just didn't make sense. You were supposed to be busy at Roller Shakes." After he nodded, jaw clenched, I continued. "And Senna...you were reaching for her soul. Was she about to die?"

He answered with a slight nod, but he didn't lift his eyes from the forest floor. "It's awful knowing you can't save someone on the brink. I could only reach her soul. Reapers are not supposed to intervene or we could accidently trap a spirit here forever. But when she survived, I ran to get help." Darkness crossed his face. "I didn't have enough time before I was summoned here."

The lingering sadness that always followed in his wake, hidden beneath his arrogant exterior, revealed his true feelings about the job. How much of his smug attitude was a mask and how much was him? Did I know the man I'd almost kissed at all?

A shiver stole through me as the dampness settled deep into my bones. Even my wolf's fever couldn't warm me from the chill of impending death. I was trapped side-by-side with a reaper, waiting for our kidnapper—the killer—to return.

"I've known reapers before. Miss Raven was one before she retired from The Calling." An awkward laugh escaped me. I needed it to release the tense emotions that had built inside my lungs. "Now she runs the workout studio in town and uses her experience with death to scare soccer moms into step aerobics class." We allowed ourselves a quick chuckle to relieve the tension. "Oh, and I guess you actually used *The Book of Prophecies* for the recipes like you said?"

That earned relaxation in Crow's jaw and slight gratitude as he lifted his brow in acknowledgment. "Yeah. Except it was a flop. I should have known it was mostly soups and stews. Not exactly fried diner foods." The moment of lighthearted conversation darkened when his frown returned. Despite the grim situation, I couldn't shoo away the question that kept popping into my mind.

"Why did you hide that you're a reaper?" I asked, curiosity nagging at me though I knew I should be delving deeper. *Why is Gemma trying to kill you? And me...? And better yet, what are we going to do when she gets back?*

Crow came as close to me as the summoning lines would allow. An invisible barrier of powerful magic stopped him a foot from the edge where the soft earth was dug out. "Because someone's stalking me." Another sigh puffed out of him. "I was hoping you could reinstate the protection spell, because it's what I came here for. I've been sent threatening notes since I first became a reaper."

My gaze flickered to the woods around us as goosebumps pricked the flesh across the back of my neck and down my arms. "Do you think Gemma is the stalker?"

"I was afraid it might be her, but I have no proof. I ran from Lake Tahoe, changed my name, and got the last job anybody would expect an angel of death to have."

"Running a roller rink?" I almost smiled at the contrast between a disco ball's shine and Crow's grim Calling.

His fist dug into his pocket until he produced a crumpled piece of paper, stained and looking as though it'd been folded and refolded dozens of times. "This was left on the windshield of my car after my first reaping." Carefully, he peeled the paper open and held it up to show me the scribbled words.

You will suffer as I have suffered. And after your loved ones are taken from you, you're dead.

Sudden weakness threatened to buckle my knees, and a weight anchored in the pit of my stomach. The curve at the bottom of each letter "Y" looked as familiar as the too-short "Ts." I closed my eyes, drawing on a memory. Had I seen the handwriting in *The Book of Prophecies? No. It looks like the note at Senna's.* The letters matched.

Crow continued, oblivious to my epiphany. "I can't blame people for hating me. To them, I'm the one who takes away their loved ones. And I was awful at staying hidden when I first started reaping, which means someone probably saw me and wanted revenge."

"Crow." I stepped forward, but the magic stopped me, my body freezing about a foot away from the summoning lines. I shuffled back a pace and pointed at his pocket. "I recognize that handwriting. I think you're right—Gemma was the one stalking you. I've heard reapers don't usually get many details about the spirits they guide, but do you know if you might have reaped the souls of Gemma's parents?" The information came back in bits and pieces like a jigsaw puzzle with a near-complete picture. Hattie had said Gemma suffered the loss of her parents to a hit-and-run car accident.

Before he could answer, the crack of a broken twig snapped our attention to the trees. A huff followed, and the dim moon-light glinted against the shiny barrel emerging through the fog.

"Very smart, Wolf." Gemma gleamed. She stepped from the shadows as the mist swirled and dissipated from her movement and body heat. Murderous intent revealed itself in the squeeze of her grip at the gun's trigger and in the sparkle of her eyes. "Truly a mystery writer. Sett was right about your skill with solving crime." With a twitch of her lip, the ghost of a smile flickered across her face. "Too bad it won't save you now."

Steadily, she kept the barrel of the weapon trained on me as she kept her distance from the summoning lines. Despite the thrashing heartbeat in my ears, a glimmer of hope ignited within me as the pieces of the puzzles fit together. Once I understood her, we could reason with her. We could draw her close to the summoning lines where her footprint could break the line and drop the barrier, then I'd shift and lunge at her with heavy paws and werewolf speed, knocking her free of the weapon and pinning her into the mossy mud.

Or maybe that was merely wishful thinking, given the satisfied smile that twisted her face.

Gemma glanced at Crow. "You will suffer as I have suffered, and you will watch as I kill someone you love." When she returned her focus to me, she flicked off the safety and curled her finger over the trigger.

CHAPTER 20
BACK TO HIS FUTURE PART II

STARING down death had a clarifying effect. Much better, in fact, than standing next to the angel of death. Crow merely distracted me as my heart ached for him and his Calling.

With the weapon pointed square in the middle of my chest, a thousand thoughts rippled through me. Life may have flashed before my eyes, but it was too fast for me to recognize. Instead, my mind settled on only one memory—a mundane moment at Mockbuster when I stood beside my best friend and discussed Gemma's life.

Her parents were killed in a hit and run, and Crow must have been the one to reap their souls. Had she seen him? *You will suffer as I have...*

My hands shot out in surrender. "Wait!" Though she didn't stop, she didn't shoot either. Hesitating, her finger hovered over the trigger.

Her head tilted, and anger rippled over her pursed cheeks. The smooth ponytail was disheveled for once, with flyaways framing her face. "Be quiet!"

Despite the mask of rage, the pungent and intense ammonia that wafted from her told me she was far more afraid than she was angry. She'd killed and attacked before, but was shoving Fate into some wires and a swift whack to the back of the head the same as meeting the victim's gaze at the end of her barrel? Fear's stinging stench rippled in undulating waves as her arms quivered. Eventually, her tense muscles would give, and she'd have to drop her hold. I just had to make it to that moment and then draw her closer.

"Just tell me if I'm right," I said, trying to pique her detective's curiosity. "Just tell me if I'm really as skilled at solving as Sett says. Give me that before you do anything dangerous. Please..." My voice died away. The darkness inside the barrel seemed to swallow me, but I cleared my throat and continued with the time I was given. I pointed at Crow. "You saw him at the accident."

A flicker of confusion showed as she blinked. It matched the brief pineapple pizza scent. Finally, a smell better than fear's stench and anger's burn boosted my courage.

"At the car accident where you lost your parents. Did you think Crow was the driver who hit them?"

"Curse my Calling," Crow swore in reaper terms, cursing his grim work.

She licked her lips and glanced between us. I followed her gaze to him. "But you weren't the driver, right?"

"No!" he answered with the soothing scent of truth. If only Gemma could smell it. "I've never been in a car accident. Not even a parking ticket on my record, I swear."

A strange half-laugh, half-scoff escaped our attacker. Gemma shook a flyaway hair from her face and white-knuckled the weapon. Her feet shuffled slightly.

"Crow was there because he's a reaper and he helped your parents' souls find rest," I explained, still biding my time until her arms would fall.

Gemma's head shook, sending more flyaway hairs floating

across her face. A few strands stuck to her wet lips. "No. No, he crashed a stolen car into them. Then he just walked away so he wouldn't get caught. When I tried to follow him, he disappeared. That's when I knew he must be a magician or warlock or whatever the hell you creatures are called." Her narrowed gaze slid to him, and she spat. "You just walked away like their lives were nothing!"

"You're wrong!" I nearly bit my tongue trying to pull the words back in. It was the truth, but it was impulsive and stupid to shout at a woman with a loaded gun. "Listen, Gemma, Crow is a reaper, not a warlock. He guides dying souls to the next life. That's why you saw him at your parents' car accident. He disappeared because The Calling shrouds him, right?"

Crow's curls fell into his eyes as he nodded. "I was brand new at the job then, though, and terrible with the shrouding."

Her mouth twitched, but she didn't deign us with a response.

I sucked in a breath, trying not to look at the cold, hollow barrel. "You're waiting to kill him because you want him to first lose someone he..." I felt awkward saying *love*, but she'd seen us nearly kiss. She'd known we shared a date because he'd arrived early that day and with a rose in hand for me. Crow was all alone in Bewitcher's Beach with a changed name and no friends or family. He'd created his own witness protection program. From what Gemma knew, I was Crow's closest loved one. *I* was the target. "You want him to lose someone he cares about because you felt he took that from you. So you removed the protection spell's power over Bewitcher's Beach and then chased him here and destroyed the pages all in some long plot to get revenge on the man who you believed to have killed your parents."

"I didn't remove the spell's power," she said, irritation furrowing her brow. "Someone else must have done that, and I was merely the lucky one. I avoid dealing in magic. Though I have to admit, summoning has been helpful. When I followed Crow here, the protection spell's power was gone until *you* had to meddle." Her voice was sharp, but her narrowed eyes were sharper and fully fixed on me now. "You and that witch and warlock. Thankfully, the warlock led me right to the pages, and I burned them. I had to stop Fate from recreating the protection, and then Senna too, because I was not about to let their annoying little project ruin my chance to show Crow how it feels to lose someone. And of course he wouldn't leave the boundaries of Bewitcher's Beach if the spell was back. I was racing against time when I wanted him to suffer longer." A strange, hollow laugh escaped her. "But honestly, I should thank whoever destroyed that stupid protection magic in the first place. I wouldn't have known how."

I didn't have time to dwell on the bad news. "This isn't the way to deal with your loss—"

"Shut up," she growled through gritted teeth, but I didn't listen. And I wouldn't stop while the smell of fear still came from her. I wouldn't give up while that hint of stinky hope still filled my nose.

"It hurts," I said, suddenly slammed with a weight on my chest though she'd yet to pull the trigger. Thoughts of Christopher flooded my mind. Warm memories of his smile and of our shared love of movies and rock metal music. Grief rose at the most unexpected times. "I know it hurts."

"No," she interrupted me, but I returned the sentiment, speaking again before she could.

"I lost my husband, and it hurt more than anything in the world. It hurts so much, but that's when we..." The clean, refreshing aroma of curiosity's peppermint mingled with an array of other emotions. Gemma stared at me, but the anger had fallen—the mask had fallen. She waited, almost eager for my response as if I had the secret for dealing with grief and the loss of a loved one. She was a mirror of me, lost without her family. Her anger and the blame she threw at Crow hadn't let her move past the accident.

When we what? What could I say? I'd had no family to turn to when Christopher died. I had four kids to care for and a worn-down RV. We'd traveled the state, searching for a place to settle down, when Christopher got sick and the silver in the antibiotics had killed him. Soon after his passing, I found Bewitcher's Beach. I'd found Hattie haunting Everland Theater and ran into Sett after Barney filed a noise complaint against my pups.

Since then, Hattie had always been there, a loyal best friend. She was always ready with a harsh word to keep me in check and plenty of encouragement to counteract it. Since then, I'd spent movie nights with Sett and tasted his delicious home cooking. Since then, the kids had grown to consider Bette their cousin and Sett a father figure. Even Mae had taken the role of a pseudo-grandmother to the pups.

Tears filled my eyes, and my throat tightened. "That's when we turn to those who are still here. Those who care for us, our, our—" I cleared emotion from my throat so I could say the word. For too long, I'd been pining for my previous pack, the family I didn't know and couldn't remember when my loved ones were all around me. "Our pack. Like Sett. He cares for you, Gemma." My voice choked, and the smell of vanilla washed away all of Gemma's anger and fear and wiped the grimace of revenge from her face.

Glowing movement flashed behind her, but I didn't dare break the fragile gaze we shared. Still, I knew that the glittering gold in the forest was the manifestation of my best friend. Hattie was here, and the mere thought of her help—of the woman I considered a sister—sparked the rise of tears. Gratitude flooded me. From the corner of my eyes, I caught the shadow of Sett's frame. The tip of his wings and horns and broad shoulders moved through the mist. To my relief and surprise, he moved the fastest I'd ever seen before. It was then I noticed his muscular wings were flapping, carrying him through the trees.

My pack had arrived.

The smell of burnt toast wafted from Gemma, mixing with the scent of the love that filled my heart. Her arms finally dropped. She held the gun limply at her side, shoulder slumped in defeat and regret when a blur of glittering gold and a glowing, pale light surged toward us.

The ghost swept through the woods in a flash, dashing directly through Gemma. Her thin manifestation moved just enough wind to knock the can of Diet Pepsi from the summoning line. The open can toppled to the ground, spilling. The moss quickly soaked the fizzing soda like a sponge. Gemma gasped from the icy chill of Hattie passing through her, and the weapon fell from her hand with a thud.

All at once, I was free, and I turned to the only one still trapped. I kicked the boxing gloves away from the summoning line and found myself throwing my arms around Crow. I collapsed into his hold as he reached for me.

Sett landed in front of Gemma with a smash against the earth, all stone and serious intent. Straightening, the sheriff kicked her weapon away. He yanked handcuffs from his belt and marched toward her.

"You lied about Miss Knovel's fingerprints," he said gruffly, and Gemma didn't respond. She didn't need to. "Gemma Stone, you're under arrest for the murder of Fate Kalabar and the attempted murders of Senna James, Noema Wolf, and Crow." He continued reciting the rest of the rights as he stepped behind her and secured the handcuffs around her wrists.

Finally, I allowed myself to breathe freely and sink into Crow's hold. His wiry strength matched my weighted relief, and he held me into him where his pulse beat in his chest. I smelled every bit of his citrusy happiness as he enveloped me in his arms.

"I'm so sorry I got you into this," he breathed. "I had no idea she would consider you...consider us..."

"Just say thank you," I said, meeting his gaze.

The usual mischievous smirk found its way to his lips again. "Thank you, Miss Mystery."

As he said it, my focus shifted over his shoulder, and I locked eyes with Sett. I rarely smelled the gargoyle's emotions since his reactions were blocked by all that heavy stone, but I didn't need a scent to understand him. Instead of the scent of rain, I witnessed a flash of sadness in a brief wince and the flicker of a frown.

He turned and guided the culprit into the trees, but not before I caught another look—a look of hard lines in the clench of his jaw and narrowed eyes. Was it jealousy? Or determination?

Or perhaps regret for having canceled the Ghost Pirate Moon. Stars glittered the sky, but the forest was dark, darker than the rest of the month since it was only two nights until the New Moon. Our chance to celebrate with the ghosts was nearly gone. The joy of a holiday that we so desperately needed after another murderer had torn through our town was almost out of reach. I could never recover the burned pages and bring magical protection back to Bewitcher's Beach.

Despite the heavy sky's reminder of my failure, my spirits lifted as Hattie came to my side and Crow flanked me. My best friend's gaze flicked between me and the stony shoulders in front of us.

I burned hot and pretended to ignore her knowing look. For now, I wanted to bask in the comfort of the pack that surrounded me. Though the little family I'd found in Bewitch-er's Beach was enough for me, a twinge of worry struck my gut as thoughts of Stevie's plea came to mind. I still owed my children a holiday celebration that they likely would not get the joy of experiencing.

CHAPTER 21
A NEW HOPE

TWO DAYS after Gemma's arrest and the storm's end, I resolved to find a way to make a miniature version of the holiday for my kids. Madam Rowena must have caught wind of the murder and summonings here because nobody had heard from her. At least not since Senna called her from the hospital for an extension on her school project.

Still, I held onto hope that the Madam would brave Bewitcher's Beach and recreate the spell with Senna. And thankfully, the uncertainty didn't stop Bewitched residents from preparing. They took to the cobblestone streets and cleaned up the mess of broken branches, torn awnings, and toppled benches.

We didn't have the protection spell or the ghost pirate reunion from the Drunken Oyster, but we had each other. Even with the murder solved and the storm over, Bewitcher's Beach still had a lingering chill of worry wafting in the air that surely made Sett and Fitz hesitate to invite the pirates to shore. Fitz always did whatever the people wanted, and though they wanted a holiday, they wanted safety more. Safety I couldn't give them since Gemma had burned the spell.

Instead of a ghost ship, the sun made a grand entrance with warm rays of yellow light beaming through thin clouds.

Side-by-side with Hattie, Bette, Mae, her husband Wallace, Noodle and family, and more, we filled trash bags, raked leaves, and righted what the storm had turned upside down. Mae kept the morning lively with plenty of gossip as her tiny dog ran through the park, yipping and nipping at Halen's shoelaces until Stevie talked the pup down.

The briny scent of the sea returned, and the sun broke through fluffy white clouds. Even the wind settled to a gentle breeze as the town itself seemed in need of a moment's relief. After all, Bewitcher's Beach had lost its protective blanket and witnessed the first tastes of danger and destruction over the last couple of months.

I brushed curls from my face, which gathered a bit of sweat from my forehead to my hand. I wiped my palm against my jeans and smiled as Bette floated after the pups in a round of Ghost Chase, a game they'd invented where she surged forward and spooked them until they fell into a fit of laughter.

Hattie and I threw around ideas about hosting a pirate-themed dinner at Everland Theater, but the built-in rows of seating didn't leave enough space for the traditional pirate games.

"It just won't fit even if we open up the stage, and I'm not about to let half the town traipse across my stage!" Hattie said, hair swishing as she shook her head. "What about the library? Didn't you say Judy wanted more eyes on it to drum up interest in books?"

My wolf ears flicked forward, alerted by the idea. "That's genius, Hattie!" Hattie used one finger to flick hair away from her face. A small smile curled her ruby lips, and she lifted her chin.

Once Gemma was arrested, Judy was released. Though livid at times and perhaps too attached to her hoard of books, the librarian was responsible for nothing more than scaring a few patrons who hadn't returned their rentals on time. Oh— and hiding her scheme to make a show of summoning. She'd intended to have Fate and Senna disappear from various places around town just after they announced "I'm off to the library, because books are magic and knowledge is power, just watch!" The plan was guilty of being cheesy, and though no harm would come of it, Sett ultimately had Judy call it off after the use of summoning in Gemma's attempted murders. "Since Judy isn't getting her magic show, maybe she'll want to help us plan a pirate party. She can include history books and the swashbuckling series for kids!"

Overhearing our plan, Mae bustled toward us. She scooped her yapping dog into her arms and scratched behind its ears with her claws as she raked her eyes over me and grinned with one eyebrow piqued. "I wouldn't worry too much about replacing the holiday. A party might be in the works as we speak." Her red dragon's eyes glittered with the gossip she so desperately held back.

"What do you know, Mae?" Hattie asked.

She sucked in a breath and blew out a puff of smoke from her nose. "Nothing. Oh, except that Sett made Judy agree to work off her anger issues at Miss Raven's exercise studio."

"Speaking of Judy," I said as I waved my pups to come to the bench where I'd taken a break from cleaning. "You two chat; I'm going to make a quick visit to the library." First, I intended to apologize to Judy for having jumped on her. Then I'd present the idea of bringing books to a pirate party.

At the library, the smell of old books filled my nose and joined with the faint scent of *The Book of Prophecies*. Rose perfume, cinnamon bread, and wool yarn mixed into a strange and comforting aroma, just as it had the first time the grimoire called to me. The pups headed for the left side of the library where the children's books were stocked on shorter shelves. A basket of puppets and felt toys filled the corner, and small round tables covered the open space. In the center of each table, cups of crayons sat atop stacks of coloring books.

When the kids disappeared to hunt for a new read, my attention turned to the front desk. I sucked in a breath to slow my pounding heart as I forced myself to walk up to Judy, who hunched over a box of records that she was carefully reorganizing. Today, the librarian wore glasses with the frame in the shape of a snowman's bottom. Atop the round base, through which Judy peered at me, a black top hat balanced on two stacked circles. She adjusted the glasses as if the lensless frames could help her see me more clearly.

Though I felt the need to run, claws didn't grow and no fur popped up on my skin. Maybe I finally had a handle on my panic even without the protection spell.

"I—" My voice came out squeaky, as if I'd become the little mouse and Judy the crab with the snapping pincers. I cleared my throat and began again. "I wanted to apologize for jumping on you the other day." Judy pursed her lips, creating a sharp line along her angular cheekbones. It wasn't a response, but she didn't stop me from continuing either. "I hope you can forgive me. And I realize you're not a fan of movies because they're not books."

"They certainly are not," she quipped and leaned on the desk with her elbows, interlacing her fingers in front of her.

I offered her the best smile I could muster. "Books truly are amazing. I was thinking, when people rent particular movies, I can recommend a similar book they'd enjoy."

"The library doesn't need your pity charity."

I nodded and said, "It's not pity or charity. It's a mutual relationship. All stories are still stories no matter their medium."

She stayed silent, but the sneer had nearly wiped from her face now. Was she considering taking the olive branch? Finally, her tongue clicked, nearly identical to the sound of Sir Crabby's snapping pincers. "I happened to hear *you* might need the charity, though."

I tilted my head, a natural canine response that always came out in the most awkward of times. At least now I wasn't face-to-butt with Sett's stony behind.

Judy continued, busying herself with sorting the index cards in the records box as she spoke. "A little half-dragon may have mentioned that you and Hattie are hoping to fund a remodel of Everland Theater."

She wasn't wrong, but it wasn't a secret either. We'd been planning to bring the big screen to Bewitcher's Beach for quite some time.

"So," she said as she pulled off her glasses and stared at me with all the intensity of a woman on a mission. "I suppose I could offer a helping hand to the theater by way of Mockbuster. I was thinking, since we lost our beautiful pirate celebration, I could host a holiday party at the library with both books and movies. Anything pirate or family related. And I suppose similar movies can be matched with books for recommendations. But I'll be running the event and absolutely no food within the library, so if you could…" She paused to wave her hands, gesturing generally around her. "Plan some sort of beach bonfire for snacks and treats or something—"

"Done," I said, my heart swelling. I extended a hand across the desk to seal the deal with a shake.

"We do not interrupt in the library," she said, correcting me. She stood, the thick ruffles of her skirt falling to her ankles, and she took my hand. "See to it that you do not interrupt me—or jump on me—again, and we have a deal."

We shared a firm shake, and I couldn't help but smile. Maybe it wasn't too late for us after all.

"Well." She clasped her hands in front of her and swayed back and forth on her heeled boots. "My hope is that this event will make up for what I have lost. Of course, Senna will no longer be doing a summoning demonstration with me to spark interest in books. It would be in poor taste."

"Of course," I agreed with a mirror of her serious expression regarding the topic.

"Did I hear my name?" a voice said brightly.

Judy shifted her gaze to the witch who skipped up to us. The bandages on her head were gone, and she was returned to her fashionable, cheerful self. A sparkling smile spread across her face, and her hair was wrapped in a crown braid. Her cropped floral T-shirt matched flowery ankle socks that were intentionally bunched at the top of her white sneakers and beneath the wide hem of her high-waisted jeans. "Healed, I presume?"

"That's right." Senna beamed. "So are we talking about recreating that protection spell, or what?"

My eyes almost bulged right out of my skull. A flourish of hope bloomed in my chest, and I nearly wagged my behind as if in my wolf form. I had to admit, the thought crossed my mind, but I wasn't ready to suggest it to Senna or dare tinkering with spells on my own. Not while the trauma with the summoning spells was still fresh in everyone's minds.

"Really?" I couldn't help it. "Is that possible? I mean, you're not worried someone will try to stop you?"

Senna shrugged. "Lulu didn't become a legend by being afraid."

"Did you get it approved by the council?" Judy asked.

"Sheriff Lawrence is the one who suggested it," Senna said as she dug into her little leather purse and pulled out a ruby lipstick. After she swiped it over her lips and made a little pop with her mouth, she pointed at me with the stick. "Also, the sheriff mentioned helping you track the origin of that one prophecy you were talking about. I think I can use it in an essay for my final graduation project to the head witch." Tears stung my eyes, but I sniffed and quickly blinked them away. Senna tilted her head and told me to follow her. "Anyway, I was sent here to summon you."

My ears folded back as Judy and I exchanged a nervous glance—confirmed by the hint of ammonia in the air between us. Summoning wasn't a happy topic around Bewitcher's Beach lately, especially for the poor witch who'd suffered a scary blow to the head.

Senna's eyes slid back and forth until she grinned sheepishly. "What? Too soon to joke?" She linked her arm through mine and told me a surprise was waiting for the brave wolf who saved her life. My cheeks burned because the honor wasn't mine to accept. Doctor Pitt had taken care of Senna's injuries. I'd merely gotten lucky when I suspected Crow and stalked him through the woods. I couldn't imagine the pain the reaper must have felt every time he was called to the dying and unable to intervene.

Thoughts of Crow lingered as Senna led me and the pups to Roller Shakes. The giant tilted milkshake on wheels was a beacon for hungry kids. Dio and Halen darted ahead, shouting about what they planned to order from the menu full of fried foods and sugar while Stevie and Jovi argued which milkshake flavor was superior—vanilla or strawberry. Senna opened the door to the rink, and the first two boys ducked inside while I called for Jovi and Stevie to hang behind.

I waved to Senna that I'd catch up with her in a moment,

and she shrugged. "Okay, but don't take too long, someone's waiting." Her eyes sparkled with mystery.

I nodded and then crouched in front of my son and daughter, who looked at me with impatient eyes. "I'm sorry we didn't get to celebrate the Ghost Pirate Moon. I don't know if we have any family beyond the five of us—"

"Can we go inside now? I'm starving." Stevie interrupted me as she unfolded her arms and pointed to the door. Squeaks released a loud squeal in agreement, making Stevie giggle.

"Let me finish. I just want you guys to know that I'll keep looking for our family, but I can't promise we'll find them. Or that we have any."

Jovi shoved his glasses up his nose and stepped forward, placing one hand on my shoulder. "Mom, I'm just glad you're okay now."

I glanced between them and noted their scents of banana cream pie mixed with citrus: excitement and happiness. "You're not sad about the holiday?"

Stevie's little shoulders rose and fell. "I just wanted cake and pudding and games. Can we have cake and pudding and games here?"

"Of course!" A laugh escaped me. I suppressed a knowing grin when Stevie turned and yanked the door open, disappearing inside the noisy roller rink. I'd been so obsessed with finding family that I never stopped to ask what it was my kids really wanted. "And I promise I'll still be on the hunt for any cousins or aunts or grandparents you might have out there somewhere."

Jovi leaned forward and wrapped his arms around my neck for a quick hug. "That's cool, but I feel like I have too much family with Dio and Halen already." With that, he turned and followed his sister.

Though I was left alone on the steps, I'd never felt less

alone in my entire life. Pure joy smelled of fresh lemon lime, and I suddenly had a hankering for a cold can of Sprite instead of a Diet Pepsi. I stood and pulled the door open. As soon as I stepped on the carpet of swirling purples and blues, somebody ambushed me.

"Surprise!"

CHAPTER 22
WEEKEND AT ROLLER SHAKES

A TINY SMELLY dog licked my face when Mae untangled herself from the sudden hug. Squeaks chirped his protests at the poodle for having snuck a lick of his face too. It took a moment to get my bearings and understand that Mae was welcoming me to a party at the roller rink.

Twinkling lights decorated the café, and "A Pirate's Life for Me" blasted from the DJ's booth. Black wreaths with wire ships hung over the skate rental desk. A large wooden plank balanced on a crate in front of the rental area. Kids teetered along it like a game of "walk the plank" to retrieve their skates from the attendant. The colorful rink had been transformed into a pirate's getaway, but the skulls on the black flags weren't what caught my attention.

Dio laughed and pulled on skates. Halen jumped around him, poking him with a plastic pirate hook. Stevie nestled herself into a booth between friends from school and dove into a giant bowl of cake topped with two huge scoops of ice cream. Jovi was happily marching to a quiet corner with a book from the kids' swashbuckler series that Judy had recommended. The scent of lemon and lime tingled in my nose as happiness swelled.

Hattie surged forward with a mischievous grin on her face. "Apparently, Mae *can* keep a secret. She knew this was planned even when we were trying to figure out the logistics of throwing our own pirate party."

"Oh, Honey." Mae slapped her hand to her chest where she fiddled with the collar of her fuzzy wool sweater. "I keep *plenty* of secrets." The scent of lavender wafting from the half-dragon confirmed this was the truth. "I couldn't very well ruin the surprise this was intended to be for Noema." She patted my arm, smiling with a flash in her eyes. When the little dog squirmed, she walked away, busy wrestling with the yappy pup.

The surprise?

Sett ducked underneath a rope of lights strung from the skate rental desk to a tall machine that dispensed game tokens. The smile on his stony face made the smell of Sprite stronger. He held up a loaf of bread wrapped in plastic. "The sourdough I promised you."

"Halen will go nuts for this," I said as I accepted the gift, and we walked to the center of the diner to look for an open booth. "I'll have to limit his sandwiches so he doesn't eat it all. Thank you, Sett."

He chuckled and offered to make a second loaf, but I waved it off. It felt good to talk as friends again, but I couldn't imagine what he was going through after having to arrest Gemma.

"Are you doing okay?" I asked as I peeled away the plastic wrap and ripped off a section of the crust. The spongy sourdough sparked my taste buds, and I held back a delighted groan.

"About as well as you, I'm guessing," he said. I furrowed my brow as he continued. "Gemma confessed that she tried to blame Judy when Judy started looking suspicious. And"— he cleared his throat—"she also confessed to targeting you since you're close to Crow. Anyway, I think the whole town needs a little holiday fun. Even if we can't visit with the pirates.

"Madam Rowena called. She's on her way, but she said not to get our hopes up considering the Drunken Oyster is supposed to appear tonight and she might not make it in time. Once Senna told her a little bit about the protection spell, Madam Rowena warned me it'll probably take way too long to piece together and cast. So we're enjoying a party at the roller rink instead."

"Do you know who put this together?"

He ignored the question and leaned close, pointing to the skate rental desk. Though kids dodged around us and conversations buzzed, for a moment, it was just the two of us standing among the joyful chaos—and Squeaks. "I found roller skates that actually fit me," Sett whispered as if it was a roller rink conspiracy against men with big feet.

The scent of vanilla filled the space between us, whether from me or him or the loving way Squeaks was peering at the sourdough loaf, I didn't know. I leaned into Sett for a hug, soaking the cool feel of his chilled skin as our arms touched, when Stevie interrupted us.

"Mr. Sett!" *Tsking*, Stevie crossed her arms over her chest. "You promised you'd skate too, but you're still in shoes."

Sett's slate eyes crinkled in the corners, and he shot me a look that said "help me". But it was too late. My daughter had wrapped her little fingers in the sheriff's hand and was already dragging him to the skate rental desk. He glanced over his shoulder, stricken with pretend fear, and I lifted my hands in a shrug. "You're a goner!"

Bette waved to me from the center of the rink. She floated and danced beneath the disco ball, half the town skating and stumbling around her. The place was packed from wall to wall with chattering townspeople.

"Look at what's playing," Hattie said as she caught up with me. She nodded at the screen mounted above the skate-fitting counter. On the TV, Westley and Princess Buttercup from *The Princess Bride* were falling down a hill together. I laughed, as I always did during this scene. "This was all Sett's idea."

I turned to her, processing what she'd said. The man who'd just lost his friend and coworker had planned a roller skating party for the entire town? "Sett?" I repeated.

"That's what I said, isn't it?" She scoffed and waved her transparent hand right through my ear. "What's the point of your wolf hearing if you don't listen?"

I shook my head. "Always with the blunt truth, Hattie—"

Before I could finish, Crow appeared. He interlaced his chilly fingers through mine and tugged me toward the front of the skate rental line. "Let's get you laced up," he said with a wink. "I happen to know there's a couple's song coming up on the DJ's queue."

"Is there?" I asked as I nudged him with my elbow. "Feels like a high school dance all over again." Not that I remembered my high-school years, or who I may have danced with. I only remembered Christopher, and that was enough.

"I thought you didn't become a werewolf until you were an adult," he said, looking at me with a furrowed brow. Crow didn't know me as well as most of the townspeople, but he wasn't wrong.

"True. I have no idea if I even went to high school, or if I had a date, or where I lived, or—"

"Who cares?" he said, waving my words away. "You know where you live now *and* that I'm asking you to the prom."

As soon as the skates were secured on my feet, he offered to help me stand and tugged me toward the rink. We passed Hattie, who laid a ghostly hand through my shoulder.

"If you need more blunt truths, I'm team sourdough," she whispered.

I ignored the comment but couldn't help looking over Crow's shoulder as we half-skated, half-danced in the center of the rink. My gaze landed on the man who'd arranged the whole event. Sett stood beside Hattie and Bette at the edge of the rink. They chatted until Mae joined them with her husband and enough steaming mugs of cocoa or coffee for half the rink in her claws.

Senna and Judy had also arrived, gathering in the circle on the side of the rink. They each took a mug and sipped while kids darted around them.

I skated—terribly—while surrounded by friends and family. When my lanky legs tangled and I fell, Crow reached out and caught me or Stevie skated up beside me and held my hand. Too often, the wheels had me slipping and sliding, even with Crow's support during our "couple's skate" song. The Backstreet Boys' song "As Long As You Love Me" blared through the speakers, and dozens of paired-off skaters went round and round hand-in-hand. When the song faded away, I excused myself and stumbled toward the rink's exit to join the pack of people gathered at the edge.

My pack.

They waved me over, and Hattie surged forward. "Madam Rowena is here!"

Sett offered a hand to help me step off the wooden floor and onto the carpet, where my leg slipped out from under me. He cupped my elbow and helped me straighten as I pulled my feet beneath me.

"She's here?" I repeated.

Sett nodded calmly. "Senna is already outside speaking

with her. I thought it might be helpful to share what you remembered of the spell as well."

"Of course." I hurried to remove the roller skates. The Drunken Oyster might make it to shore. If we could get Madam Rowena the information she needed in time to cast the spell before midnight.

Outside, a gentle breeze swept my curls over my shoulders while I greeted the renowned witch from Shadowvale. Madam Rowena was all class in a burnt orange pantsuit that complimented her brown skin. Shoulder pads puffed up the suit top and gave her an air of superiority. The fashion was beyond my realm of understanding as I stood there in my scuffed mom-jeans and old Jon Bon Jovi T-shirt with an oversized brown sweater wrapped around my waist.

Nervously, I accepted Madam Rowena's hand for a shake. This was the person we'd been waiting two weeks for. The woman whose expertise was the life or death of the beloved once-in-a-decade holiday. The only witch around for miles who might be able to truly cast complicated intention magic like the protection spell.

Madam Rowena clasped her hands and addressed us. "From what Senna here has told me, I must admit, I have not come prepared. This spell will take far too much preparation, and that is only if we have the correct order and pattern. It sounds like it's a great possibility that the pattern may be misre-membered." She glanced at Senna, who frowned. "But I bring good news for both Senna and Bewitcher's Beach. I have a temporary protection spell that can be cast over the length of a football field for twenty-four hours. If you'd like—" Her long lashes flicked as she slid her gaze to Sett and Mayor Fitz.

When had he arrived? Of course the mayor wouldn't miss something as important as this. And wherever a party occurred or happy people gathered, the little bald man with his perpetual smile always appeared. "I can cast the temporary protection for a one-day celebration with the pirates. Senna has agreed to help me with the temporary intention magic to make up for the days at school she has missed. And rest assured, my student will not go unpunished for the secret she kept regarding her classmate. She will be expected to work hard studying *The Book of Prophecies* for any help it may offer to recreate the true protection spell. If she keeps up with this, her credits will be reinstated for the rest of this school term, and she'll stay on as a student at Shadowvale University."

My heart soared, and the delicious smell of banana cream pie swirled around me as excitement buzzed between us. Finally, Sett shook her hand and sealed the deal.

Let the Ghost Pirate Moon holiday commence!

CHAPTER 23
CLUE

THE WAVES LAPPED against the shore in calm, rhythmic sweeps, reaching like long foamy fingers to the tips of our toes. Townspeople shuffled in the sand, eager to be the first to spot the Drunken Oyster on the horizon. The temporary protection spell lifted everyone's spirits, and the swell of citrus, mint, banana cream pie, and vanilla mixed as happiness, curiosity, excitement, and love wafted from shapeshifter children, vampire teenagers, and elderly dragons alike. Not a single Bewitched dared miss the joyous celebration of the midnight sighting.

Someday, we'd get the true protection spell back, and each and every day would feel as safe and secure as tonight.

Bonfires crackled with orange and yellow flames that licked higher and higher as half-dragons poked the logs with heat-resistant hands. Children chattered enthusiastically between quiet giggles. They discussed what the pirates would wear, what types of swords they'd wield, and how grand the ship might look. As they huddled just close enough to the fires to keep warm against the midnight chill, Sett crouched beside them. He told tales of brave pirates who survived raging storms for a chance to see the Kraken with their own eyes. Jovi shook his head in disbelief while Noodle stood on his tentacles, eyes bulging and mouth munching on a bit of salted beef. Halen shoved Dio when he gasped, and the two started a back-and-forth elbow brawl until Sett calmly interjected with his arm between them.

"Now, don't be alarmed," he said, capturing the attention of the roughhousing boys. "When the ship draws close and the ghosts glimpse us here, you might see a few of them pass on, which means their spirits will drift into the sky like lost balloons. But don't worry, they're happy. Many of them simply wait to see their loved ones here one more time before they can move on."

A bitter laugh came from Cliff Conflick who floated as a fuzzy apparition behind Sett. As a guy who was murdered here only weeks before and was now trapped in town, Cliff was clearly envious of the pirate ghosts who were able to pass on.

The casual bump of Crow's hand against mine drew my attention away from the grumpy ghost. Tingles spread up my arm from the contact and I swore I caught Crow smirking and glancing my way before he checked the silver watch on his wrist. The watch's hour hand—that I now knew was shaped like a scythe to match Crow's Calling—ticked from eleven fifty-nine to midnight.

All at once, the lively conversations ended, and the entire beach went silent save for the unfurling of the frothy water over dark sand.

The lighthouse's wide yellow beam stopped its endless spinning and then went out, leaving us in scattered darkness. Only the flickering blaze of the bonfires lit the beach until the faint glow of a ghostly ship appeared on a tall wave. Collectively, we kept our breathing on hold and only sucked in the salty air when the black flag raised on its mast.

Silence burst into joy. Every Bewitched cheered, clapped, and raised hand-sized flags, waving them in the gentle breeze to greet the ghosts. The Drunken Oyster eased closer to the shore with the wave that crashed and rippled toward us. Though the people surrounding me snacked on salted beef, biscuits, and beans, I only smelled my own excitement, and it made me crave a delicious fluffy pie.

The ship's flag billowed in the briny current. With the glow of the ghostly boat, the symbol of the skull and crossbones looked lit up from behind. The summoning and skating were over, but the skulls had arrived, and I couldn't help but wiggle with joy like a wolf wagging her tail.

With Mae, Hattie, Bette, Crow, Sett, my new friend Senna, and my children gathered close, I couldn't feel any happier. Curious about my ancestors and the life I'd had before becoming a werewolf—but not happier.

Little gasps echoed from the children who witnessed the Ghost Pirate Moon for the first time. I joined them as ghosts surged ashore, laughing and arguing and rushing past one another to mimic hugs with their loved ones. Dozens of Bewitched greeted their great-great-grandmothers and long-lost ancestors. Even Judy cracked a smile when her great-aunt floated over the sand with a serious expression that mirrored the librarian's harsh face.

I scanned the beach for any sign of a pirate with a sword as if I could recognize the woman mentioned in the chosen witch prophecy. "Which one is Annette?" I whispered.

A ghost froze and blinked as he rubbed his long scraggly beard. "Annette, ya say?" My cheeks burned after realizing I'd said it aloud, but I nodded curtly. "Annette the Threat?" He chuckled, revealing gaps in his teeth. "Why Captain Annette has gone and said goodbye to us Drunken Oyster ghosts." His wispy arm lifted and pointed to the night sky, where a glowing ball of light lifted into the stars. "She's moving on to calmer waters now." With that he gave me a little dip of his chin and floated away.

My heart sank but only for a moment as it was buoyed by a gentle touch. Rough fingertips brushed over my elbow, and a chill rushed against my back. I twisted to see Sett offering me an apologetic smile.

"I'm sorry Noema. I know what meeting her meant to you."

Beside him, Hattie nodded as she untangled herself from a hug with another ghost. Any shred of sadness was swept away as I stood between Hattie and Sett with Crow and Mae nearby. I smiled and assured them it wasn't a big deal. "Honestly, if you could smell me right now, you'd know I'm not the least bit disappointed. All banana cream pie goodness over here," I said, swirling my finger in front of me. It wasn't the whole truth. I caught a whiff of pineapple pizza as I glanced between Crow and Sett, both flanking me now. Thankfully, nobody else could smell my confusion as I stared at the two men who took up equal space in my mind.

Senna had dressed for the occasion in a fashionable pirate-themed outfit with a billowing blouse and a red sash tied at the top of a long black skirt. She grinned and agreed with me. "This is so exciting! Who is going to tour the ship with me?" She raised the wooden tankard of rum and egged Crow to knock his cup against hers in a toast.

I had to admit, the Drunken Oyster was intriguing. Our ragtag crew of werewolf, witch, reaper, and gargoyle hiked through the sand. We smelled curiosity's peppermint until it was quickly swept away in the building breeze.

If this were a movie, we might decide to sail out to sea together like an unlikely group of friends looking for adventure. The thought had me giddy to return to my notebook and jot down a pirate-inspired screenplay idea.

The chilly water soaked our feet and ankles as waves undulated over the shore and we eyed the ghostly ship up close. With the wind picking up fast, the waves grew stronger and threatened to pull my feet out from underneath me. Sett shouted over the crashing waves for us to head back, but it was too late.

The undertow and my unsteady gait on two legs got the better of me. If I'd had any energy, I could have shifted to all four paws and found my balance. But the late midnight hour and the anticipation of the holiday left me taxed and stuck in human form. When the forceful rush of the receding wave pulled me off my feet, my arms flew out to grab Crow. I missed his reach and slipped into the water. After a moment of thrashing in the cold water, strong hands lifted me from the sucking wave, and I found myself looking into Sett's slate eyes.

My wet scoop-necked sweater slipped off my shoulder. A gasp escaped Senna, who stood beside the sheriff.

"Noema!" she breathed and pointed at my torso. Sett's brow furrowed and his gaze darted away in an attempt to afford me privacy, but it didn't last. His eyes flicked back to my collarbone, where everyone else in the circle now fixed their attention.

Had my shirt fallen off in front of the whole town? Heat burned my cheeks and chest, and when I dared to look down, my breath quickened.

The soaked sweater still covered my chest and stomach, but right there on my exposed shoulder and collarbone, a mark appeared. As if a tiny artist was inside of my skin, a shape bloomed on the flesh like a drop of ink spreading across paper.

Breath left my lungs. I twisted my head to get a better view of it, smashing my neck into multiple chins. The mark filled in until the ink stopped in the sharp shape of horns, or perhaps pointed ears.

"The prophecy," Senna breathed. "You must have been related to Annette, and when she passed on, you finally received your mark."

Could it be? Gingerly and with a shaking hand, I brushed my fingertips over the mark. Hope bloomed within me. The storm was over, and a whole new world was on my horizon as if I were a pirate setting out to sea. The mark of the prophecy was on me... *me*! A thrill rushed through me like a wave just before it crashed.

I was chosen, which meant long before I'd become a werewolf, I'd truly belonged to a family of witches. It also meant the daydreams inspired by the grimoire's smells were not daydreams at all. They were visions.

I met Senna's gaze. If she were right, I was a witch. I was both a werewolf who couldn't remember her past, and a witch who would tell the future...

Join Noema for another enchanting mystery in *Apparitions, Aerobics, and Arson: Book 3 of the Bewitcher's Beach Paranormal Cozy Mysteries!*

Please consider leaving a review at your favorite place to purchase books! Also, a share with your friends who love to laugh and solve mysteries would be greatly appreciated. My quest as an author is to make others feel seen through the adventure of fiction. Please reach out to me and let me know if my stories have touched you. You, dear reader, are who this book was written for.

BEWITCHER'S BEACH
RECIPES

STEVIE'S SURPRISE COOKIES

When to eat: at a party. These are rich, colorful, and perfect to bring to a potluck, birthday party, or Ghost Pirate Moon celebration. Kids are sure to love them, but be sure to swap out any chocolates from this original recipe if serving to werewolves!

Ingredients:

- ¾ cup flour (all-purpose is recommended)
- ¾ teaspoon baking soda
- ¼ teaspoon salt
- 1 cup rolled oats
- ½ cup unsalted butter (softened)
- ⅔ peanut butter (creamy, not crunchy)
- ½ granulated sugar
- ½ cup brown sugar
- 1 teaspoon of vanilla extract

- 1 egg
- 1 and ⅓ cups of any combination of treats: peanut butter chips, peanuts, M&Ms, Reese's Pieces, semi-sweet chocolate chips, white chocolate chips, macadamia nuts, rainbow sprinkles.

Instructions:

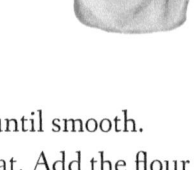

- Preheat the oven to 350 degrees F and line baking sheets with parchment paper.
- Combine flour, baking soda, salt, and oats.
- In a separate bowl, combine butter and peanut butter and beat until smooth. Add sugars, egg, and vanilla and beat. Add the flour mixture and stir in any combination of treats.
- Scoop ¼ cups and shape into balls.
- Bake for about 10–13 minutes, or until the edges are browned.
- Once fully baked and cooled, dig in!

SETT'S SIMPLE SLOW-COOKER BEEF STEW

When to eat: during a storm, when it's cold, or when you want to clean only one pot. Between solving murders and hiring enough help at the police station, Sett has gotten too busy for extravagant dinners. This simple stew is his winter-time go-to.

Ingredients:

- 2 pounds of beef stew meat in 1 inch cubes.
- ¼ cup flour (all-purpose)
- 1 teaspoon salt
- ½ teaspoon pepper
- 3 cloves of minced garlic
- 1 teaspoon paprika
- 1 and ½ tablespoons Worcestershire sauce
- 2 and ½ cups beef broth
- 8 ounces of tomato sauce

- 1 onion (diced)
- 3 gold potatoes (peeled and diced)
- 3 carrots (peeled and chopped)

Instructions:

- In a large freezer or resealable bag, add flour, salt, and pepper. Add meat. Seal and shake.
- Add the bag's contents and the rest of the ingredients to the crock pot. Stir.
- Cook on low for 8–10 hours.